Rose

J. Olsen

Rose

Acknowledgements

Thanks to Stephen Matthews at Ginninderra Press
for generously supporting his authors.

Particular thanks to Kate O'Donnell, Abigail Nathan, Dalice
Trost and Susan Trost for helpful, professional editing advice.

For those who fight domestic violence

First published 2018 by
GINNINDERRA PRESS
PO Box 3461 Port Adelaide 5015
www.ginninderrapress.com.au

Contents

Main Characters — 7
1 Ladies — 9
2 Vice — 17
3 South Australia — 22
4 Julia at Home — 29
5 Meetings — 35
6 Kate — 46
7 Walk in the Forest — 51
8 New Girl — 57
9 Simple Lessons — 67
10 Phone Call — 74
11 Eagle — 81
12 Pigs — 85
13 Jeremy — 92
14 Casework — 100
15 Forever — 109
16 Thief — 115
17 Home Visit — 121
18 Admission — 131
19 Visiting Holly — 138
20 Leaving — 145
21 Lee's Threats — 151
22 Kate's Threats — 156
23 Lisa Charles at School — 161
24 Kate Visits Lee — 165
25 Giving Shelter — 170
26 Jamison — 176

27 Orphan   181
28 Marlene   188
29 The Mare   189
30 Lovers   196
31 Night in Rose's House   201
32 Lisa Charles   207
33 Winter Clothes   214

Main Characters

Julia Honeychurch (teacher in special unit)
Brian Honeychurch (husband)
Claire Honeychurch (their daughter, four)
Ben Honeychurch (their son, five)
Bonnie (their dog)

Dr Kate Selby (lecturer)
Rose Cavanaugh (girl in Julia's class)
Lee Cavanaugh (her stepfather)
Holly Cavanaugh (her mother)
Debbie and Deedee Cavanaugh (Rose's sisters)
John & Marge Cavanaugh (Lee's parents)

Bob Richmond (principal of the school)
Ruth McGill (secondary teacher in Julia's unit)
Peter Clark (boy in Julia's class)
Jason Barker (boy in Julia's class)
Jeremy Gatewood (school psychologist in Julia's unit)

Mel Davidson (ranger and Jeremy's friend)
Lisa Charles (police officer)

1

Ladies

East of my home lies a grey forested ridge, brittle gum and red stringybark in the middle of the city. Each Thursday I climb the ridge to sit with my back against a tree and wait. An ant drops from my shoe and jinks along through dried leaves, a goshawk sails a noiseless course between smoky limbs. A faint flow of thunder from the east carries thoughts about people – promises not kept, thin white hands, the murmur of her voice and the shape of her eyes.

They told me not to feel any disgrace and maybe I don't. Maybe it's a good place to sit and wait and decide.

And then there was the rain. After weeks of cerulean sky, the downpour came in sheets over the city, trickling down strips of bark in the arms of ribbon gums. Faces crowded in foggy bus windows as children left their houses. The smell of dirt and wetness came in gusts through the door as Julia sat in her yellow-lit classroom.

Jeremy left muddy footprints on the carpet. With a field guide under his arm, he'd come in smelling like eucalypt and baby powder. He loomed over Julia's desk in his white shirt and black vest with his hands apart as he talked. 'I've got it.'

Julia didn't look up. 'I don't care, Jeremy, but you're going to tell me anyway.'

She glanced out the window at the dark slanting rain. A white limo rushed by with a V-shaped aerial on its boot. Damp fallen leaves slapped up on its tyres.

Jeremy pushed his wire-rimmed glasses up onto the bridge of his nose and caught her looking out the window. In a quiet California drawl, he murmured, 'Here's what we do.' He looked down and scrunched his forehead, trying to remember details of a plan to change the circumstances of some malicious no-hoper in their care, mix birdwatching and damaged children in a single stroke.

Julia picked up a pen and rearranged papers on her desk. As he rambled, she glanced around the bone-coloured room at lessons and charts and lists of rules that were laughed off by any boy capable of mounting a thimbleful of decent reprisal. Peter Clark had taped a drawing over his desk of a stick figure with an angry crooked line for a mouth standing on a rooftop shooting dotted line bullets into a crowded street.

'Jeremy, you're a school psychologist, not David Attenborough, and you'll sound a little defensive if you spring that on them. You're an indoor worker.'

'No, no, you miss the point, you don't understand –'

'Oh, I understand. It's a little naïve, a little simplistic, isn't it? They'll laugh at you, Jeremy. Try to understand something: you Americans come from Puritan stock, we come from criminals.'

Ruth knocked on the open door and looked in. 'There's a file you need to read for Thursday's meeting.'

'Come in.'

She marched over and slapped the folder on Julia's desk, 'ROSE CAVANAUGH' was written in tall red letters in the border.

Ruth opened the file, leaned over Julia and tapped her finger on the top paragraph. 'Read this. Welfare wants her in your class, Julia. Quick. Some question of being fiddled with by the stepfather, but they can't prove it. They're pressuring us, and I don't like it.'

'Who?'

'Who do you think? The office. The people who don't have to live in this zoo.'

'So what's new?'

Ruth frowned. 'I still don't like it.'

With Jeremy and Ruth looking over her shoulder, Julia tracked with her finger down a bland list of psychometrics and euphemisms about Rose Cavanaugh – 'bloody shirt,' 'beatings with a strap,' 'dysfunctional family,' 'weapons,' 'police record,' 'stealing' – and testimonials from teachers arguing that Rose Cavanaugh needed to be saved. This always meant, 'out of my class into your special unit.' Appended were dated observations, stories about trouble she'd caused at school, how teachers blamed these episodes on her wretched home. She had released all the prize-winning budgies from a neighbour's cage and teachers saw that as a clear metaphor; Julia smirked and shook her head.

Ruth tapped Julia's shoulder. 'Animal libber. You and Rose can break into the national zoo together and free some tigers.'

Julia turned the page. 'She nearly burned down the school by setting fire to her desk. The class was out to lunch.'

'Call for help,' said Ruth. 'We had any girls who set fires?'

'No,' said Julia and sighed.

'I've got things to do,' said Ruth, and she left.

Julia looked at Jeremy. 'What do you think?'

'I met her mum, Holly I think her name is, and her stepdad Lee, the evil one who they say is molesting her, and I gave Rose some tests.'

'What's she like?'

'Rose or Holly?'

'Rose.'

'Quiet, thin kid with honey-blonde hair. I watched her on the school playground before testing her. She meandered, you know, didn't talk to anyone, didn't look at anyone, just drifted and looked suspicious.'

'And?'

'But this one's very mistrusting. After a couple of minutes, she came round the corner of the building and surprised me, on purpose I think, to say, "I know what you're up to."'

'She's coming in for sure, isn't she?'

'We have no choice,' said Jeremy. 'The office will break my head if you try to keep her out.'

Julia nodded. 'Girls have the same rights as any boy to come into this place and learn how to curse at teachers, steal from the local shops and have sex under age.'

'It'll be rubber-stamped at the meeting,' said Jeremy. 'Count on it. Anyway, I'm off.' He left Julia alone in her room.

The following morning, Jeremy came back and talked about his plans for compassion, how they would save the new girl from a cruel family and the unfeeling primary school that had rejected her.

'That doesn't help Peter Clark very much, does it?' said Julia.

'Peter Clark? What are you talking about?'

'Peter Clark, red hair, snotty nose, bad breath, too many head colds. Big square teeth, in my class, and in your care. Remember? Has a drawing taped over his desk about killing people. You're the school psychologist.'

Jeremy looked down. 'I'll spend time with him today, maybe walk to Haig Park and talk with him.'

Peter Clark, thought Julia, was the sort of ten-year-old boy that Lewis Carroll hated so much. A murderously red face under curly red hair. Some teachers rumoured a vestigial tail, but the evidence was slim. He was simply a child raised by parents unfairly kept back by their lack of talent, so they blamed Peter. Julia wondered if there was a biological theory about survival rates of red-haired boys in refined society. His freckled face that flamed when he tantrumed and beat his chair against the wall.

'Let's work this out,' she'd said to him.

'This place sucks.'

'You're right, Peter – it sucks. I'll help you with the first one.' Julia touched him on the shoulder. 'Forty-five times six. Tell me first, what's five times six? Like we did yesterday.'

She watched him darken, lower his brow, jut his big lower teeth, 'It's stupid. I can use a calculator. Tables suck. So do you.'

'One day, Peter, you'll write me a letter and say, "Thanks, Mrs Honeychurch, for forcing me to do maths when I was in Year Five."'

He didn't smile and she rested her hand again on his shoulder. 'You need tables to go to a bigger school, get out of this one, and so the checkout chick doesn't rip you off.'

'I'll go back to my old school today, away from you.'

Seamless performance, thought Julia. Grown men had used that one on her more than once. And Peter was a skilled technician who studied Julia's hands to see if she twisted them around her sleeve or hid them shaking in anger behind her back while her voice stayed calm. Gotcha.

Before lunch, Julia said to the class of four boys, 'You've earned a run outside and a game of cricket.'

Peter looked up. 'Do I need a coat?'

'That depends, Peter.'

'On what?'

'On whether you want to be warm or not.'

Dialogue like that every day, she thought, and parents don't understand why we crack.

On the oval again it was Peter: 'Who brought the fucking ball? Dickheads. I remembered the bat. Who brought the fucking ball?'

'You're the dickhead, Peter,' Jason Barker staring squarely into Peter's rusty face, stepping closer and pushing him over.

The others laughed.

Peter struggled from the ground onto his knees, pushing himself up with the cricket bat. 'You prick,' and he swung the bat at Jason's head.

Julia heard wood cut the air near Jason's mouth. Jason wrenched out of the bat's arc.

'That's enough,' she said. 'Pick a number between one and ten. I'll decide who bats.'

They glared. Too much at stake now to back down. Peter swung at Jason's head again.

He dodged the shot, smiling into Peter's face, leaning forward and yelling, 'Seven.'

'Try again, Peter.'

Peter, ready to lower Jason's IQ with the bat, spat out, 'Three.'

'The number was four. Peter, you start. No more fighting or we go inside.'

Close to lunch now, only ten minutes more, Peter stood up from his desk and walked to the door to sharpen his pencil. He rammed Jason's blond head into a book. A giggle, a burst of chatter, and Julia felt herself bristle. Muscles tightened in her chest, she strained to hold in 'You little bastard!' The others watched to see what she would do, see if she would perform like a pro, and she did.

She calmed her voice and spoke slowly. 'Peter. I asked you to help me out today.'

He grinned and let Julia know she'd lost.

'Why did you do that?' she asked.

A brainless question shaped by three hours of serial defeats. What did she expect him to say? 'I momentarily lost my head'? He paid no attention and continued to smile with that winning freckled face. A skilled tormentor. A wild animal had climbed up inside of Julia, scratching and demanding to be fed. Heart thumping in anger, she murmured, 'Don't lose it.'

Placing her hands on the desk, she pushed back her chair, stood up and said to the boys, 'I want you to work quietly for five minutes.'

She turned and stepped from the room and walked into Ruth's class. The boys feared Ruth, a stout middle-aged Scot with no waist and broken capillaries in her face. At times, Julia used Ruth to lever herself back over the ledge to sanity. They listened to Ruth all day through the wall, watched the window vibrate when she screeched. Her voice sounded like a car alarm. Her six boys sat in desks facing the four walls.

'Can you watch my boys?' said Julia. 'I won't be long.'

'Everything okay?' said Ruth.

Julia nodded. 'Fine.'

'I'll look in every couple of minutes.' Words for Julia's boys, not Julia.

Fred lifted his face and looked up, the others kept their heads low and wrote.

'I won't be long,' Julia said. She'd said this twice now, inadvertently displayed her edginess.

As she walked out, Ruth watched Julia's reflection in the window opposite as she approached the ladies' room and stiff-armed through the swinging door.

Inside, she could smell perfume. A teacher from the main school must have come over and dabbed something on her throat or wrist. A fluorescent light flickered over the mirror. It needed to be changed. Julia's steps echoed on cream tiles. She pushed open the cubicle door, stepped inside, turned and locked herself in, leaned against the side of the cubicle, pulled her long dress to her waist and slid her hand inside her pants.

She listened to herself breathing, opening her mouth slightly as she thought about Kate, remembering an afternoon last week when they drove to the river in her car; Kate was quiet from work and stressed. They sat holding hands and Kate turned and said, 'Take off your clothes, except your knickers.' A gentle command with no force in it. She found, looking back, something that aroused her, leaning against the wall in the cubicle. Kate touched Julia. They rocked and held each other for an hour. Julia listened to the river wash against her lover's voice.

Julia remembered what they did after that, slipped a shirt on and waded in the river. The shock of icy water on their ankles made them suck air in; they moved out further until the water rushed around their thighs and they joked about somebody coming down the road and catching them.

Julia stood in the ladies, floating out of the school, stiffening her legs, and whimpering.

She sat down, limp on the toilet seat with her dress pulled up, breathing hard with her eyes shut, close to sleep.

After two or three minutes, her eyes opened slowly. She gazed at the bare cubicle and tiled floor. The fluorescent light still flickering. She stood, tugged at her dress and stepped out the cubicle door. Her fingers twisted the handle and she rinsed her hands in the basin.

Julia turned from the basin and dried her hands under the machine, adjusted her skirt and blouse in the mirror, took a brush from her pocket and stroked her hair. She pulled open the door to the ladies' and walked down the hall to her classroom.

Ruth stood outside Julia's door with her arms folded, a sentry. Together they looked over the boys and Julia smiled.

'Been good?'

'Very good.' Ruth strolled back to her room.

Julia touched her own cheek with the back of her hand; tension had gone out of her face. She walked to Peter's desk and looked down at his book. 'You finished a whole page.' She rested her fingers on his shoulder as he looked up and curbed a smile.

2

Vice

Elegant gulls arch their throats. Pairs of female lovers beg copulations from passing males then raise their young without him.

Lee Cavanaugh came in glassy-eyed with his hair tangled. He tilted into Holly Cavanaugh's face and whispered, 'What's this fuckin' mess?'

'What do you want?'

'I want the place clean. Got it? Clean.'

His rancid breath blasted her face and caught in her throat. She stepped back and looked down to vomit, held it in and said, 'The girls. There's not enough money.'

Lee squirmed and sat on his anger. He squinted into her bowed head, the tangled limp hair at the edge of her face. He waited but she didn't look up. 'Fuckin' pathetic. Look at you. Look at me when I talk to you. I'm fuckin' out from six in the morning till six at night fixing people's fucking blocked toilets. Six in the morning till six at night for you and the feral little bitch. What the fuck do you do?'

'Don't.' Her eyes slid up and watched a string of oily hair slide off his skull and dangle in front of his ear. Red veins patterned his hands.

He backed against the grey laminex table they'd bought to match the cupboards, orange vinyl chairs, scuffed linoleum under faded orange bench tops. A cupboard with sliding glass doors divided the tobacco-coloured kitchen from the lounge room. Holly kept her best glasses there, and the china dishes for visitors to use. An orange patterned blind covered the window above the kitchen sink, a window that looked out over the backyard and Hills hoist and the spindly brown lawn that nobody watered except the two dogs.

'What? What was that? Didn't quite catch what you do.'

She saw him through the blue reek of cigarette smoke, then she couldn't look at him any more.

'Let me review my first point,' he said. 'That was a bit quick for you. I'll go slowly. I'm fucking tired of carting you and this fucking family around like dead weight. Any man would be pissed-off. Any other man would leave. What do you do all day? You don't fix yourself up, a glance in the mirror shows that. If I'd only had a crystal ball ten years ago and seen what you'd look like at thirty-four.'

'This makes me tired.'

'Bullshit. I'm the one who's tired, tired of you being a pig. You don't take care of yourself. There's nothing in this house worth looking at, the fridge is empty.' He reeled back, trying to keep her in focus, like a dancing cockatoo.

Holly thought he would stop soon. It was midnight.

'In short, easy words: keep the house clean, keep yourself clean. You're a pig. The house is a cesspool. Repeat that back to me.'

Dirt under his fingernails, in the creases of his knuckles swung towards her. She ducked.

He leaned back, fist in her face. 'Another thing. That vice you gave me for me birthday.'

Holly hunched down.

'Look at me. I asked you a fucking question.'

'Don't know what you mean.'

'Where'd it come from?'

She studied the floor with brown hair in her eyes. 'He's trying to catch me out,' she thought and said, 'Why?'

He exploded. 'Because I asked you, that's why. Tell me how you got it. The little bitch-clone lifted it from a neighbour – right?'

'You wanted it, so we got it for you.'

'Look, I know you steal things, the cops know it too. We all know you steal things and take Rose along, teach her the trade. Goes back at least three generations in the female line, doesn't it? Now, one more time, where'd it come from? Someone's car? Someone's garage?'

'Be careful what you ask for.'

'What?'

'Be thankful we got you something. You never remember her birthday.'

'Of course I don't. She's not mine – she's yours. Six more years, and like magic, she vanishes. Gets the boot.'

'You adopted her.'

'Bullshit. Where'd the vice come from?' Lee reached down, turned his trouser cuff, and pulled a short knife out of the top of his boot. He leaned down and tapped it on the laminex table. Tap. Tap. Tap.

'I told you,' she said. 'I bought it.'

'You don't have any money, unless you're on the game in Mitchell. Teaching her the trade, are ya? Come on, where'd you get it? Tell me before someone gets hurt.' Tap. Tap Tap. In the face of stubborn women, Lee believed in one simple rule: threaten harder. Or try extortion. 'Right. Your choice. I'll get it from Rose, drag her out of bed. She'll tell me.'

Lee spun on the heels of his boots and stepped into the hallway. He could feel Holly's bony fingers cold and clutching at his back, tangled in his shirt.

She spoke into his back, 'I'll tell you. Don't touch her again. Never.'

'Where'd it come from?'

She wavered.

'Tell me where the fucking vice came from and we'll get along fine. Fact is, I don't know if I really want to know where it came from.'

'What do you want?'

'Nothing. I'll get it from Rose,' and he twisted away from her fingers hooked into his shirt, and charged towards Rose's room.

The knife bounced white light off the bare bulb in the kitchen. He could feel Holly drag at the back of his shirt.

With a hard little fist, she braced her feet sliding along the carpet. 'No, I'll tell you.'

He stopped and turned to face her. 'Where?'

'Come back so we don't wake Debbie and Dee.'

'Tell me.'

'Yes.'

In the kitchen, Lee sat on a chair. 'Where?'

'At the hardware store.'

'You didn't buy it. You don't have any money.'

'I was wheeling Debbie in the stroller.' Holly paused.

'Debbie? What's Debbie got to do with it?'

'I checked around to see no one was looking, and stuck it under Debbie, put it in the stroller with the nappies and bottle and things. I just wheeled it past the guy at the counter.'

Lee's eyebrows knotted together, his jaw slackened in mock confusion. His wet mouth started to crack. 'You what?' in a squint. 'You mean, you nicked it from a store?' His eyes started to shimmer.

'Yes.'

'You stole it from the fucking store by sitting Debbie on it?'

'Yes.'

Lee jerked back and roared. She could see every filling in his head; the tassel of hair swung back and forth over his ear. 'You silly bitch.'

He laughed again. 'Maybe you're not that silly. Lift a ten-kilogram vice into a baby stroller and wheel it from a store. Ha-ha-ha! Rose's idea, I bet. You're not bright enough to think of anything that original. I think the kid's teaching *you* now. Is she?'

Holly looked into his face and said, 'Don't touch Rose when I'm gone.'

Lee whitened for a moment, looked away.

'Leave her alone,' said Holly, 'or, I swear, I'll take the kids and leave.'

He folded his arms tight across his chest, then forced a low, growling chuckle. 'That little whore. Nasty little bitch. Reached that age, hasn't she? Making up lies to cause trouble. And you're stupid enough to believe anything. Well, no one else is stupid enough. She's a little whore and you're no better.'

Holly watched him, Lee on the back foot now. 'Keep your hands off Rose. Touch her again, I'll tell the police.'

20

He sat up on the bench, betrayed by white in his eyes. He wiped the palms of his hands on his overalls. 'Go ahead. Who'll feed your brats then? What shit. You won't go to the police, even if…if I was doing what she says. Tell the little whore to shut up if she wants to stay in my house.'

A child, probably Debbie, started crying in the dark hallway, down past dirty cream walls with no pictures or decorations except children's handprints, and some of Lee's.

Holly stood hunched and tired with sad, red eyes. She turned to the door. 'Debbie's crying. You woke her.'

He bounced off the bench to the kitchen doorway, between Holly and her daughters. She turned sideways and slid between him and the wall, quivering as he passed, expecting the blow to the back of her head as she started down the hallway towards the bedroom and two small girls.

Rose Cavanaugh stood inside the door, listening, barefoot. She turned to shut it and padded back to bed. She lifted the covers and slid one bare leg under the sheets, then the other.

Fifteen minutes later, it was quiet. She lay back and looked at strangers floating in the room. Patterns and faces on the ceiling and walls, ghosts from the red moon, and the trees whipping in the breeze outside. Eyes wide in the dark, she saw angry faces in the crowd, and the face of a young girl.

She pulled out a notebook and wrote down what Lee had done to her.

At school the next day, Rose picked a fight with a boy who stood a head taller than she, beat and scratched him until his classmates summoned the teacher. Then Rose slapped the teacher.

The following morning, the boy's parents spent two hours shouting at the principal behind closed doors, phoned the minister, and moved their son to a safer school.

3

South Australia

'Oh, to find a virtuous woman for her price is far above rubies.'

Late afternoon and Jeremy tried to explain cats to Julia. 'If you have cats,' he said, 'and you move them from house to house, you can get them to stay around the new house instead of running back to the old one. There's a trick.'

'Butter?'

'Exactly. You let them into the new yard with butter on their paws. The cats lick butter off their paws instead of wandering off, and you can talk to them during that time, pacify them. Your cats will keep their heads and they won't panic and bolt.'

Julia nodded. 'Thanks, Jeremy. But if you try that metaphor tomorrow afternoon, they'll laugh at you.'

'But it's true.'

'Yes, yes, I know it's true, but I've heard better metaphors in church. See you tomorrow.'

He left.

Julia asked Peter Clark to bring up his home book. She leaned away from his bad breath and urine-smelling pants.

'Let's see. "Obeyed class rules". We'll leave that till last.' Julia rested her chin on her hand. 'And "Did what the teacher asked". Let's tick "Yes". Mind, you were a bit slow sometimes, and, luckily it doesn't say, "Did what the teacher asked the very first time".'

Peter glanced at the note, then at the corner of the room. 'If you say so.'

'We don't want any trouble at home. You'll help me out tomorrow more than you did today. Let's tick "Yes".'

He watched her, closely.

'When the other boys start to jump around and act silly, you'll help me out. How about the next one. 'Tried hard at Schoolwork"?'

His eyes skated away. 'I did.'

'Okay, we'll tick "Yes". And the next one. "Got on well with other kids"? You had a fight with Jason.'

'That was his fault.' He lowered his eyes into his freckled face and tightened his mouth.

'Peter, remember what you're working on here. If the boys stir you, look away, walk away, sing away, anything, but don't hit them with a cricket bat, or a knife or whatever you have at hand. Don't let them win.'

'They never win.'

'They win, all right. You take the bait like a trout, but a trout doesn't take it every time like you do. You want to go back to a regular school, don't you?'

'Yes.'

Julia knew full well that he didn't, that he would fight and throw chairs every day to stay where it was safe. But he obeyed an important custom – let Julia know he was a hard case.

'Okay, Peter, a "No" for "Got on well with other kids", because you tried to sever Jason's head with the cricket bat, but we're progressing.'

'You mean the knives?'

Julia thought of the row of knives locked in the top drawer of her filing cabinet. 'Haven't seen one for a while, and that's worth noting.'

'Up to you.'

'Yes, Peter, it's up to me, and quite a burden. But this gives you three "Yeses" and one "No", and tomorrow's another day. Mum and Dad won't be too unhappy with this home note.'

'He'll belt me.'

'Then you'll have to do better tomorrow.' Julia waited for the normal 'He'll beat me with a phone book, lock me in my room all day without food.' But it didn't come.

She'd decided long ago that you couldn't spend too much time worrying about dishonesty in boys. Peter would find a girl who wasn't bright enough to read his lies, a girl with a big heart who would bleed over his stories of betrayal and suffering. She would work as a librarian and feed him during the day through his long tracts of unemployment.

'So Peter, don't let the boys stir you tomorrow.'

'It's their fault.'

'Don't let somebody else write your story for you.'

He wagged his head from side to side.

'Yes, Peter, I'm boring, and it's time to go home.'

He looked at the door.

'You'll be a senior public servant one day or, given your drawings over the past week of men standing on buildings with guns, you'll assassinate the prime minister from a rooftop and be famous.'

'What?'

'Never mind. It'll be good to see you tomorrow.' Julia said this because nobody else did. Peter knew he caused the drunken fights between his parents, the broken beer glasses, bottles and chairs through windows, and Peter caused his father's boss to sack him from his last job, or so his indolent father told him.

He shuffled to the bus stop.

Tired, Julia gathered papers into her briefcase, and walked to the parking lot. The Wattle Street unit was in a disused portion of the school, so even though Bob, the principal who was never there, urged Ruth and Julia to mix with other teachers across the way, they didn't. Other teachers became enemies when boys from the Wattle Street unit beat up kids from the main school, or stole their lunch money, or took their hats or shoes or lunches, beat anyone bloody who grabbed their lunch money back. Pulled out a knife and said, 'You got a problem?'

Teacher Molly Jones had steamed across the yard one morning to defend the innocent, walked into Julia's room shaking her finger. Molly had the eyes of a bad sleeper and the morning light hadn't been kind to her. 'One of your boys pushed Jeremy Kovic into the rubbish bins. Threatened to kill him. Used terrible language. Terrible.'

Julia nodded, looked concerned, and listened carefully. 'Sorry that's happened.'

'What are you going to do about it?' Molly's voice brittle.

'I'll talk to him.'

'Talk to him? What good does that do? We can't have that sort of behaviour in a school playground, even if these kids have problems.'

'Fine, Molly, I'll deal with it.'

Julia folded her arms; there was nothing more to say. Molly turned and marched out the door.

In her Mazda, Julia turned up Neil Young as loud as it would go to soothe and freshen her as she drove along Belconnen Way past burnt stringybarks and scribbly gums reaching out from both sides of the road like witches' hands, down past the black scar where the fire had torn through Black Mountain.

A Holden full of tourists crawled in front of her with oil boiling out of its exhaust. She wound up her window and stayed back from the stink as they weaved from the inside to the outside lane. On the rear bumper, near the South Australian number plate, was a torn sticker – 'Port Augusta – Gateway to the Flinders Ranges.' Australian towns, when they had nothing to offer, claim they are the gateway to someplace, hopefully a place that does have something to offer.

Julia looked at the red dirt on the number plate, waited for the driver to make up his mind, and thought about South Australia. When Julia was young, her father, a post office worker, would deliver dictums at the dinner table, principles aimed at saving his children the pain of being taken advantage of later in life. 'Never trust a man who combs his hair across his bald spot. He's dishonest about his hair, and dishonest about everything else.' Or 'Watch carefully if the salesman tilts his head to the right when he stops to think. If he does that and drops his gaze, he's lying, he's cheating you. After years of working with the public,' he said, 'you learn a thing or two about human treachery.'

But this wasn't South Australia. This was Canberra in the 1990s, the capital, the anti-city. Few people were ever taken advantage of in Canberra. Every house had a copy of *The Satanic Verses* and nobody read Bryce Courtenay or Colleen McCullough, or watched commercial TV, or liked Riverdance, or admitted to it. They hated country music, even though it was a town loaded down with broken hearts and at least twice a week somebody said to Julia, 'The book was so much better than the film. Much, much better.'

The town had a reputation for breeding cardboard public servants living a tedious lie. Teachers like Julia struggled for affection, or a place in the group, or the moral high ground just like people did in less fortunate cities. There was no longer enough money to go around. Somebody, an enemy or a friend, wanted the same job, or the same money, or the same house or the same moral high ground that you wanted. People living in the same town, fighting each other, sometimes victorious, sometimes overthrown. The cult of blame lay everywhere. Each street had its own snarling zealot who was stealing firewood from nature reserves, or office supplies from work, or screwing his neighbour's wife, and then screaming about the decline of morals. A mantle of hate lay over the city; in that regard, it wasn't so different from normal towns.

Julia drove through Aranda to Cook, past yellow real estate signs poking up like tombstones out of front lawns.

Their house was like quite a few in the 1970s, exposed Oregon beams, split-level, and big sliding glass doors leading from the living room to the garden out the back. The clean look of white ceilings and walls with Berber carpet in the sitting room and a giant Clifton Pugh etching of a barn owl that her friends had given her when she graduated from teacher's college in South Australia.

Brian, Julia's husband, taught industrial design at the local college, a good position that he liked. But the job put pressure on an over-sensitive man working at the exposed nerve endings of Canberra's education system, sorting students into two piles – the smart went to university and the dumb didn't. Teachers assigned scores that limited dumb or work-shy students to a job, an apprenticeship, or the dole, but advanced their book-smart friends to university. Brian didn't like facing the losers who'd bent their backs over essays and books for two years, sometimes longer than two years, late into the night and on weekends, and never had a chance.

As Julia pulled into the carport she saw Brian in the garage. Dressed in a faded blue sweatshirt, black track pants and thongs, he was leaning in under the bonnet of his Commodore. Brian always had his head down, fixing parts of the car, or the plumbing, or sweeping leaves off the street in front of the house.

When they met in teachers' college back in Adelaide, Brian said that Julia had that clean diction from Adelaide Girls Grammar that he'd never heard at Elizabeth High School. One night in Glenelg, Julia remembered the warm breeze drifting onto them from the north. He told her that he'd fallen in love with the way she said words like 'disheartened.' He stood with his hands plunged deep in his pockets, and Julia watched him compress sand between his toes. The darkness had parted towards Port Lincoln and two pillows of clear silver cloud lay over the sea. They whitened as day broke. At the time, soaked in wet light off the jetty at Glenelg, Julia wanted plain, unpretentious manhood from the working class. At nineteen, a lot of her friends wanted the same.

After college, they became indentured servants to the South Australian Department of Education. Probably they could have dodged that obligation, but they sent Julia to Port Augusta, a tin-coloured settlement in red sand hills three hundred kilometres north of Adelaide. This sad little union town was full of single men that made Brian look quick and elegant. Teachers looked down on them, hung about with other teachers, didn't mix with fettlers or train drivers on the railways or mechanics at the power station. Workers stayed away from teachers, though Julia remembered how the ugliest woman at the school, a woman who looked like a short black-haired troll with a brown wart on her nose, swept a gorgeous young train driver off his feet and married him. He used to come out with them on Friday nights at the hotel and bashfully tried to belong. He leaned against the counter with a bottle of Cooper's Ale in his hand, but he didn't know much about schooling, and teachers could only listen once or twice to his lesson about how 'Locomotives use diesel to drive the electric motor. The electric motor actually powers the wheels, not the diesel engine.' The second or third time their eyes drifted towards something to read on the walls, or the double doors of the pub to see which teachers had just arrived.

Julia missed Brian enough that she had trouble eating some days. He drove three hundred kilometres north from Adelaide, or Julia drove three hundred kilometres south every other weekend, at night through sandstone villages past blonde fields of grain, until they decided to marry, probably because of the strain and expense of these long journeys.

She moved to Adelaide for two years and then to Canberra so Brian could work in the new college system set up in the 1970s. This put them away from Brian's interfering in-laws, and freed them from Thursday-night greyhound racing, Saturday morning rabbit trapping, afternoon drunks outside the Pastoral Hotel, and uncles who couldn't read. It removed them from a town where men didn't wear shirts or shoes to Christmas lunch, to a town where citizens cupped their chins and tipped their heads at originals in the Beaver Gallery, standing next to the literary critic from the *Canberra Times* who had just kicked major international butt in her column this week about the death of narrative fiction.

What a town.

4

Julia at Home

'And the lord said, It is not good that man should be alone.'

Julia climbed from her car and felt the burn in her calves and thighs from standing and walking between desks all day. Bonnie, their Labrador, loped up, smiling with her tongue out and whacked her tail against the car door. Julia patted her blonde head.

Brian looked up briefly from under the bonnet. 'Hi,' he said, but he didn't smile, 'Carburettor's playing up when she goes up hills. Toy with it until dinner. Kids are in the backyard.'

'Okay.' Julia could feel the dead frown on her face, and didn't struggle to lift it. 'I'll see them and start dinner.'

She rushed into the backyard to scoop up Claire, her four-year-old, as Ben, her six-year-old, watched. 'Hello, my darlings.' She preened Claire's dark hair, hugged her and set her back down.

Ben pulled at her skirt. 'Look what I made with Joan today,' and he pulled from the picnic table a crinkled piece of newsprint coloured with red, green and blue paint.

Joan, their child minder, smiled and watched without speaking. Julia nodded to her. At fifty-five, Joan had done this a hundred times and was unfazed.

Ben held onto her dress, 'It's you, Mummy.'

Julia picked up the painting and felt her face brighten. 'It's beautiful, darling, and so are you.' She pressed her face against his ivory skin, held up the painting with her left hand so they could admire it together.

Ben reached his arms around her neck, his fingers in her hair.

Claire, looked down, frowning and coy.

'Over here. Tell me what you did all day. Come on. You got a little burnt. We'll have to ask Joan to keep your hat on or you'll turn out old and wrinkled like me.'

Joan looked over and smiled.

Ben said, 'You don't have any wrinkles, Mummy.'

She leaned back and laughed. 'Keep telling me that, we'll get along fine.'

Ben studied his mother's face from a hand length away, and watched her mouth. The children watched her laugh.

'Come on, darlings, inside.'

With a child on each hand, Julia strode, her long skirt flapping against them.

Chicken from the fridge, potatoes, and broccoli, tossed into the microwave in stages; gravy mix in a bowl.

'Ben, you can stir, please. Claire, knives, forks and spoons on the table. Thanks, darling.'

Julia leaned down to Ben. 'Please tell your father to come in.'

Ben walked down steps to Brian and his car.

Ten minutes later and Julia stood alone in the kitchen. 'Let's eat.'

The children came running.

'Where's your father?'

'Still outside.'

Annoyed, Julia walked down steps to the garage and met Brian's back sheltering the motor of his Holden. She turned her head. She hated his pear shape from behind, the narrow soft shoulders that accentuated his tendency to waver at critical moments, mouthing words that he didn't quite mean. The half circle of curly black hair in the neck of his sweatshirt matched thinning dark hair on his crown.

The progress towards hating him came in stages and progressed through distinct junctures. It was impossible to switch back. Her decision to marry him was born out of affectionate isolation more than passion, an alliance forged in the boredom of Port Augusta. She remembered the moment she knew it was lost. The woman next door, Sandy James, was a leftover hippie from the 1960s with pale orange hair flecked with silver. It was genuine; they'd seen her naked more than once. A wooden fence between their places lined with a tall hedge should have kept them apart. But from their balcony, they could see over the barricade into her backyard. The drumming whine of her lawnmower acted like a signal to Brian; he lost some of the stoop in his back and made his way to the balcony. She would strip to her knickers, and sometimes even remove them and push the lawnmower up and down her steep lawn and sing out-of-tune songs from Led Zeppelin or Cream albums. She scratched and squealed the lyrics to 'Stairway to Heaven' because, Julia assumed, years of smoking Gauloises and cannabis had coarsened her voice. Mowing the lawn naked at high noon in summer was her idea of staying healthy, though her skin had seen plenty of sunlight and looked like tooled leather.

Julia had arrived home a little early one day and Brian lay prone on the balcony, partially hidden by wisteria, binoculars pressed to his eyebrows. He was studying something on the freckled woman with hair the colour of cornflakes as she tramped behind the lawnmower. She hiked up and down for a full minute with her breasts swaying and her arms jiggling before Brian flinched and jerked his face up to look to Julia.

'What are you doing?' she asked, and waited for him to hide behind some feeble excuse.

'What does it look like?'

'I'd better not say.'

'It's nothing.'

'Nothing?'

Sandy heard none of this, following her electric lawnmower, singing 'Sunshine of Your Love' but making up words for the hard parts. Whether she knew all the words before she'd eaten, over many years, tray after tray of warm hash brownies, was something the neighbours argued about. One thing Sandy didn't know was that she started a fight between Brian and Julia that day that would finish them.

'What's wrong with it?' he said.

'Oh, you mean, what's wrong with gazing at the neighbour through a chain-link fence with your tongue hanging out? Let's see, for one thing it's sneaky.'

'Sneaky?' he whimpered.

'Yes, sneaky. Tell me. Why would anyone watch their forty-five-year-old neighbour mow her lawn naked?'

'Why not?'

The exchange went on like that for ten minutes and they got nowhere. Julia didn't know what she wanted him to say. He was fascinated by the differences in women. And that's what hurt. Julia was hard-muscled, her legs were long, and at thirty-five, she had no grey peppering in her black hair. And this idiot needed to watch their forty-five-year-old neighbour mow the lawn naked.

Julia said 'If we had a forty-five-year-old male neighbour who mowed his lawn naked, I'd ask him to tell me the day, with two days warning, so I could leave town.'

Brian was relieved that Julia wasn't as bent as he was. To him, spying on a naked neighbour was an opportunity too big to miss. He couldn't ignore it, he couldn't let it pass. He would do it again if he thought Julia wouldn't catch him.

Julia noticed flaws in him that she hadn't noticed before – small feet, a hairy back, a belly, and the way he chewed his food when he sat across from her at the table, trapped. The blemishes corroded their marriage. She used to love him in a quiet fashion, then one day it stopped.

Leaning against the garage doorway looking at his back, Julia said, 'Dinner's ready. The kids are waiting.'

'Okay.' He didn't look up. 'Just about have this thing running. Give me five minutes.'

She walked across the lawn, up stairs to the balcony, in through the sliding door to the kitchen. 'Let's start. Dad will be here in a minute.'

She served up the broccoli, potatoes, corn and chicken, chopped for Claire. As she finished serving, he came in.

'I'll get the grease off.' He rushed down the hall and came back after five minutes.

All together now.

'Tell us what happened in school today, Ben,' he asked without looking up from his food.

'We did the letter A, and Damien tried to mess mine up so he got in trouble.'

'What do you think of that?' Brian asked.

They spoke through the children.

'I think they should be doing a little more than the letter A,' said Julia. 'He could write his name before he went to kindergarten. I wish they would teach *him* instead of the lowest common denominator.'

'But he likes it.' Brian was combative about pedagogy. 'He likes school and that's what matters when you're five.'

'No,' said Julia. 'He's six, and there are a few things that matter in school besides liking it.' Snapping at Brian across the dinner table, Julia knew her irritation wasn't about Ben's progress in school.

'Come on, loosen up,' he said, deflecting a skirmish he could never win, dodging and weaving to avoid being hit. Hard-wired to run from the sting of battle, eager to please, happy to give ground. Like a failure in nature. 'Come on, kids, let's go hit the cricket ball,' he said.

Julia said, 'I have a case meeting at school tomorrow morning. And I'm acting as student rep at the university tomorrow afternoon. Can you mind the kids?'

'Tomorrow afternoon, yes. But in the morning we have a department meeting.'

'I'll get Joan for the morning.'

Claire and Ben slid back their chairs, grating on slate, and ran for the door. Brian stood, said nothing, didn't look at her, just stood and followed his kids into the backyard.

One day, the children would look through photograph albums,

page after page of Claire and Ben, Mum and Dad with broad smiles, and Julia looking into the camera in love with another woman, a woman she would spend every day with as her children grew up; at any rate, every day she could.

She and Kate Selby would stage late-afternoon breakouts, abandon their houses, and roam. Julia could smell eucalypt on Kate as she lay on Black Mountain. Julia would tremble and dream when she heard currawongs piping in eucalypt trees. At night she would have dangerous, erotic dreams and she would squirm on twisted sheets and wake Brian.

'Nightmare?' he'd say.

'Sort of.'

Kate and Julia became night people, as if their secrets would spoil in the daylight. For a time, no one could breach their stronghold. But then, partly because of Lee Cavanaugh, they were tangled in a calamity. Police came to the house and a woman died. In nature, there's no perfect defence, one structural weakness leads to another, and defences can fall apart. They were living on a knife edge by spring of that year, hidden by trees, or darkness. Now Julia was affected by certain rooms, the smell of peppermint leaves or Kate's stale clothing. A few words could make her sweat.

It was a strange town now.

5

Meetings

Choughs roll along happily with a clear mission, weak on the wing, bumbling on their feet. They should be picked off. But they have an unbreakable defence against any hawk trying to kill them, an intelligent social order. They assemble themselves into an amoeba-like mass, and enlist helpers to fight enemies and gather food. Kidnapping is important. Kidnap helpers from the neighbourhood.

Julia failed to sleep, unsettled by frost in the air. Winter stayed late that year and bit hard. Choughs rifled through leaf litter at dawn and shook off the cold; magpies played carolling tricks in their throats. Honeyeaters left the city, but teachers stayed all winter and paid sizeable chunks of their salaries to keep warm. Lacy frost lay over dead grass in the yard, and ice-scored leaves spread over the road. Fog lay knee-deep in the street but Julia had no time to bask in the grace of winter.

'Ben, eat a little faster. Come on. Joan will be here in two minutes.'

He chose his time to dawdle – when he could see her scramble around the house in disarray, late. His eyes stayed on the TV and he said nothing.

A knock on the door, the door latch rattled.

'Joan's here and the door's locked. Somebody let her in.'

No response.

'Ben, please open the door.'

She heard him bounce out of the chair, walk to the door, and turn the lock.

Joan's voice, 'Good morning, Ben.'

'Good morning,' he said.

Racing from the front door, down the path to her Mazda, Julia forced the key into the lock. Halfway in, it stopped. Pulled it out and tried again, twisted it hard to unlock the door and throw herself into the front seat. She speared the key into the ignition. Missed it. 'Can you believe it?' Tried again. Missed again. 'Damn.'

Finally it slid in and the motor turned over. Cold. It cranked slowly. Julia hoped the battery wasn't flat. Finally the car started and she slammed backwards out of the driveway into the foggy morning and lurched over wet streets. Down Barry Drive. She watched the eighty-kilometre speed limit. Left off Barry Drive into O'Connor she arced through the maze of curved roads, between maples and cottonwoods with shapely brown trunks like a woman's thigh, beating her car towards the Wattle Street school.

They were fixing the street again; a sheet of water lay in dugout holes in front of her. A spotless white Land Cruiser crept slowly, dropping one glossy black front tire over the edge into the water, then the other, rolling through the water at two kilometres an hour. This would take forever. Julia swung around the Land Cruiser, bounced over the potholes, and splashed mud on the Land Cruiser's white fenders. The driver blasted his horn, gave her the finger through the windscreen.

Into the parking lot at 8.40, only ten minutes late.

Striding into the classroom, she glanced at the four adults hunched on students' chairs.

Bob, their principal, sitting there like a mountain, looked up at her, and said, 'Julia, we've just started.'

She smiled at him, then at Kate, and Ruth and Jeremy.

Jeremy, quiet and fallible, a strict vegetarian, was the only American she'd ever known.

Dr Kate Selby, Julia's Kate, visited once a week from the psychology department at the university to advise on casework.

'Okay,' Bob pushed on as leader, 'let's get going because I have a meeting back in the main school at 9.30. I suppose you want to talk about this camp, Jeremy.'

Jeremy looked up, surprised, 'It's, uh, I didn't prepare anything, uh, it's partly that these boys need to be out in the forest and grasslands, to feel the earth under their feet.'

'A camp, uh?' said Bob.

'An overnighter at Mount Franklin in Namadgi – so they can understand themselves better, and so we can understand them better.'

Bob cleared his throat. 'Another time, Jeremy, another time. What's happening with referrals?'

As the others crouched on their circle of chairs, Jeremy tried to organise papers in his lap. 'Uh, referrals are up, a lot of aggression out there.'

'Of course there is,' said Ruth. 'What do they expect when they gouge holes in the public service? More divorce, more money problems, more anger at school, and more referrals to us. Simple.'

'Here we are,' said Jeremy. 'River Primary has a Year 6 girl named Rose Cavanaugh. Anyone heard of her?'

The others stared at the dishevelled pile on Jeremy's lap.

'We've seen the file,' said Julia.

He continued, 'They'd like to get her in this week. Now, I can go through the referral info if you like.'

Bob leaned his giant body forward, dreading that Jeremy would squander more time shuffling through test scores. 'Just tell us what she's doing, Jeremy. Why do they want her out of their school so badly?' Bob nodded as he spoke certain words to emphasise his authority. He wore a green jumper that had been new once, thought Julia, maybe when Billy McMahon was in office. A lot of people remember where they were the day John Lennon was shot, Bob could show you what he was wearing.

They waited. Jeremy pushed his wire-rimmed glasses back onto the bridge of his nose, and continued to hunt through folders, papers and notes on his lap. Jeremy always had a mournful look on his face, like a troubled young socialist. 'She's in a fair bit of trouble,' he said in a mild, California drawl. 'Hit a teacher last week. The teacher went to the union and the union supported her. She, the teacher, won't come back to class until the minister deals with Rose. Luckily, as far as I can tell, the parents aren't too literate, so they won't make a fuss. The department knows that. She'd be treated differently if she was a lawyer's kid.'

Ruth frowned. 'What else is she doing at school? Wagging? Does she do any work? Come on, Jeremy, These schools leave out the worst bits. It's a tactic. What's the home like?'

'There's a stepdad, Lee Cavanaugh, her biological mum Holly and two sisters. Rose is from a previous relationship. Welfare has an eye on the stepdad because of rumours that he interferes with Rose. One teacher said that Rose plays up to men at school, a big purring cat rubbing up against them. She twists some men around her little finger. The same teacher said that Rose never acts straight, never acts normal when she's around men. Always vamping.'

Ruth cut in. 'How many male primary school teachers are bright enough to know what normal is? They probably see her as nice and friendly.'

Jeremy hesitated, looking down at his papers, then lifted his head to meet Ruth's grimacing face. 'These days, hardly any men teach in primary schools. Anyway, that's not the point. She's run away from school a couple times, but she didn't go home. She generally goes to Belconnen Mall and she's been caught shoplifting. The security guard just cautioned her.'

Ruth again. 'That's all they ever do.'

'Anyway, that's about all I've got.'

Ruth glared at Bob, then at Jeremy before she spoke. 'This kid's been sexually interfered with. The unit's full of boys. When a girl comes in, Julia and I wear the trouble she causes, in new wrinkles on our foreheads.' She looked at Julia. 'Well, on my forehead, not yours. Last time, all the boys started posing and strutting around. Fights broke out. How many times did we catch her in the bushes with some boy's hand in her pants?'

'Exaggerating a little?' said Bob.

'Oh? Exaggerating?' Ruth squirmed in her chair. 'Exaggerating, my foot. Think, you people. Just stop for a moment and think. What about Lara Frome last year?'

'Lara Frome, Lara Frome, remind me about Lara Frome,' said Bob. 'Can't picture that one.'

'Sure, Bob. I'll remind you about "that one". Let's start with the incident at the lake.' She turned to Julia – tap, tap, tap, her right index finger on the desktop. 'That should be a good one to remind Bob about, don't you think?'

'I don't think it's necessary,' said Julia.

'I do.' She looked back at Bob. 'We took the kids down to the lake, to ride on those pedal boats they have down there, you know, two people side by side pedal themselves around Lake Burley Griffin.'

'I know those,' said Bob. 'Great fun. Great idea for the kids. '

'Great idea, Bob. Lara got on well with the older boys, you see. Quite naturally, she went out side by side into the middle of the lake with Harry Kostavsky. Remember him, Bob?'

'He was the tall one with…'

'No, Bob, he was the short one, smooth-talking, greasy, the one who always wore black jeans.'

'Yeah, yeah, nice boy, nice boy. I remember him.'

'Ruth,' said Julia. 'This isn't necessary.'

'Sure, it is. Bob doesn't understand that we have them at that wonderful age when their bodies are starting to leak. You see Bob, Julia and I stood on the shore and looked out on the lake to see how the kids were getting along, and Lara Frome had her head down, face first, in Harry Kostavsky's lap.'

'In his lap?' Bob was confused.

'Called oral sex, Bob. The heartening thing is that she didn't do it for free, it was all for pay. And Harry Kostavsky kindly organised for her to relieve the other boys in the unit for a moderate price. His kindness showed through in the tiny percentage he asked for himself. In fact, mostly, she only had to pay him in sex, a generous offer given all the business acumen he offered in return.'

Bob sat with his mouth slightly open. 'I, uh, didn't realise.'

'No, of course you didn't. It wasn't the first time, Bob. You see, they'd been getting into each other's pants, as juveniles do, in that big concrete pipe out in the backyard.'

Bob looked out the back window. The others looked at the giant concrete pipe for diverting water under roads that squatted in a bed of brown sand.

'But you can see straight into to it.' Bob's voice was weak.

'Oh, you can now. We can all see into it now, Bob, because we turned it ninety degrees. It used to sit parallel to the fence.'

'Parallel to the fence?'

'That's right, parallel to the fence so we couldn't see what was going on. We turned the pipe this way, Bob, to stop Lara Frome and Harry Kostavsky from making money. But one parent said we turned the pipe this way so we could watch. What do you think?'

'I, uh, look, this doesn't have much to do with Rose Cavanaugh. Julia…'

'Want me to go through it again for you, Bob? It –'

'Ruth,' Julia said, 'the point of these meetings is to look at each referral on a case by case basis. Nobody can stop Rose Cavanaugh from coming in here because of what Lara Frome and Harry Kostavsky did last year.'

Kate Selby levered back in her chair and watched and listened. She studied the debates until someone asked her opinion as visiting expert. But that morning, for a second time, she grew agitated, tapped her pen against the knuckle of her thumb. She raised her hand, almost pointing at Ruth. 'We don't know that this girl has necessarily been sexually interfered with. We don't know yet…'

'Look, Kate,' said Ruth, 'I appreciate what you're saying about university studies and all that, but we see these kids and work with them every day. After a while, you know these things. Books don't help. Mark my words, this kid's been sexually abused, and she'll give us trouble. We'll be stuck with her every day while you experts go back to university where it's safe.' Ruth's face had reddened.

Bob raised his finger as if to admonish her, but put it back down. He jolted at some things that came out of Ruth's mouth, but the rules were clear – stand by your teachers in front of an outsider. Kate Selby was an outsider.

Kate reached up to scratch her nose, gather her wits. She smiled faintly but Julia could see her breathing quicken as Ruth attacked her. Kate opened her fists and lay them freely in her lap. 'Now,' Kate seemed to be thinking, 'take charge.'

'I appreciate what you're saying, Ruth. You do have a lot of experience that we in the university don't have. But we need to be careful about jumping to conclusions. You know these kids and their families are never, when we meet them, quite like they appear in the case report.'

Julia moved her hand from in front of her mouth. Kate didn't need to be rescued, but still she said, 'That's right. Teachers fib, exaggerate, make the kids and their families sound terrible because they don't want to fail with a child who's too easy, a child who doesn't have major medical or family problems. Otherwise, the failure is theirs. Jeremy, what do we know about her that's positive? What's she good at?'

For a moment they sat in a brown silence and Julia felt a stab of panic.

Jeremy, more shuffling through papers in his lap. Nothing. Then he gave up and spoke from memory, 'She likes animals, horses and dogs, and apparently she's kind to them. One teacher said she trusts and connects with animals better than people.'

'She only feels equal to animals,' said Ruth, shaking her head. 'Another disposable child.'

Bob leaned forward with his hands on his knees, looking impatient, his face growing redder, 'Okay, that's all fine, but what's the decision? We need a decision.' He looked at his watch. 'Are we having this kid or not?' He looked at Ruth, then at Julia.

'I'll give her a try,' said Julia. 'There's one place in my room. If things go badly, we'll meet again and change our plan.'

Ruth leaned back and folded her arms, tried not to look betrayed. She would complain later to Julia, after the meeting. 'That Kate friend of yours was scoring points off me. Look, it's obvious to everyone – she talks differently to you than to the rest of us, trying to show off how smart she is, trying to divide us. We should never let some bubble-headed professor divide us. Never. Understand me. Never listen to her nonsense. I have never met a university type with any common sense, never met one with honest eyes.'

Julia didn't say anything, and Ruth laid her hand on Julia's arm and continued, 'We have to stop her from coming to our meetings. She doesn't have the kids' welfare at heart.'

But in the meeting Ruth backed down. She had glanced at Bob and saw no help from him. Then, as if it didn't matter, she said, 'Okay, we'll try her. But when trouble starts, I'll remind you people of what I said.'

The morning spilled dove-grey light over the scribbly gum outside her room. Kate looked over and caught Julia staring out the window at Black Mountain. Mist was clearing from trees on the high ridges. Gullies lay hidden there, ferns and streams and cool, dark places to explore. Quiet places. In a truly wild place, everything is unpredictable, but orderly.

The descriptions of broken families and broken children continued, and Ruth and Julia commented on the progress of each child in their care. At meetings, Kate and Bob were showered with stories, some lumpy and undisciplined, others round and complete; the coherence and orderliness of the story was more powerful than accurate details and fact. A successful caseworker hammered aspects of the child's life into a pleasing shape, an ornate piece of coloured glass fired in a kiln, and this brought support and praise from Kate and Bob, the people who didn't have to stay at Wattle Street.

'You're doing great work with these kids,' said Bob.

And warm praise from Dr Kate Selby.

The conference room in the psychology department was painted in coffee brown and battleship grey; an angled shelf along one wall displayed their latest papers published in psychology journals.

Opening the door, Julia looked for Kate, but she wasn't there, only Roger Brown, the department head.

'Sorry I'm late,' she said.

'That's all right, Julia. We're talking about space. In this institution, we're running out of it, and people don't want their office in the library.'

Roger Brown had warmth and a sharp intellect, but he applied it with no common sense. Intelligent, but never wise. They talked of the time he got out of a friend's car and opened a farm gate to let the car through, closed the gate and locked it, but the gate stood between him and the car and he couldn't figure out what to do. He stood for a moment, confused about how he had locked himself into the wrong paddock.

He wore a crumpled, liver-coloured sport coat that deserved to be dragged behind a vehicle at a dog track.

Julia looked at the eight men and four women, specialists on the human condition who would surely know how to cope with the stress of shrinking space in the department. None did.

Kate walked in. She had changed out of the pants suit and jacket she'd worn at the school meeting into a navy polo shirt and cords. Her black hair was combed back and wet. She smiled and nodded, and Julia felt a moth flutter low in her belly.

The air tasted sour, as if people had been incinerated in the room. She'd apparently walked into a fight and the room was stuffy with the bad breath of angry people. Then it was on again.

'An outrage,' said Ralph Turner, 'a complete outrage. I teach psychology, this is the psychology department, our staffroom is here, and you send me across campus. Executive decisions made in the last six months are an abomination. We'll stand together and fight.' Ralph Turner spat indignation into these meetings to reduce his anxieties about feeling commonplace. He sat up and searched for support, his mouth tight, eyes flashing with anger or maybe the pain of insult. He opened his mouth to say something smart, then closed it again.

Nobody looked at him; they gazed at the agenda on the table in front of them, or talked to each other, or stared ahead.

A strict rule of status in the department decreed that senior lecturers, associate professors and professors each had progressively bigger offices than did low-borns, and this distinction was counted in bricks. Lecturers had offices two bricks longer than tutors, senior lecturers three bricks longer, associate professors four bricks longer, and so on. Prime rooms, gifts to the high caste, had a window looking out on the parking lot so they could watch for the parking inspector. Cuts had disrupted this ranking and some even had to share a room.

'My work has been dramatically affected,' said Ralph Turner. 'I have two papers to finish and I can't get time on the computer.' He ran his hand through his hair.

Ralph was a preacher. Sadly, his personality disorder barged in and ruined the flow of his lectures. Students had trouble understanding why he studied left-handedness in galahs but preached social constructionism – there was no truth, he said, because each culture invented its own. Ralph had a bumper sticker that read, 'Subvert the dominant paradigm', which made students laugh because social constructionism was the dominant paradigm. He creaked with conservative dogma. The Australian government paid him and he sniggered at fools who didn't see the Australian government as an enemy nation, an occupying force. Unlike the younger students, Julia was full of interior rules that checked her from standing up during lectures and charging him with hypocrisy. When students giggled and whispered behind their hands, Julia felt sorry for him because he couldn't help it.

Roger Brown said, 'I hope this isn't slowing the publication of your findings on left-handedness in galahs.'

The group twittered and giggled.

A short balding man said, 'You're so consumed in battles over which foot galahs hold their biscuit in, Ralph, you forget your wife's birthday.'

A perfectly manicured woman in a deep red suit sitting next to Kate smirked at Ralph. 'Aren't you discussing your book *Taxidermy and Gender* on the *Book Show* this week?'

The group burst into loud guffaws and Julia wished their psychology lectures were this interesting and not packed with qualifiers like 'possibly' or 'that raises more questions than it answers'. They lectured about cooperation and altruism and principle, the rights of women, the war against hunger, famine, injustice. They loved humanity but didn't like people very much.

Kate smiled at Julia, flooding out their whining voices. But then they came surging and fussing back.

Ralph was beside himself. '…and I, for one, plan to lodge a strong protest with the vice-chancellor and tell him exactly…'

Julia tuned out again, for the second time that day gazed through the window, prowling over Black Mountain. A light breeze had cleared mist from the summit. She hunted over the ridge, through gullies, over streams into forest and didn't return to the voices and faces in the meeting. Reaching into her handbag, she pulled out a notebook, laid it in her lap and planned a nourishing meal for Benjamin and Claire.

6

Kate

Julia found her way to Kate's office. Kate stood talking to a student who looked about nineteen, with red hair and batting lashes, a pink glow in her cheeks.

'That was a really interesting lecture, Kate,' said the student, and 'I'm really enjoying this unit.'

Kate displayed an artlessness that drew hungry young women to stand at her door and waste her time. She had that polish that sneaks up under the guard of the semi-educated. She was big, raw-boned, thirty-five, with black hair, green eyes, good to look at, and she seemed not to understand that. She always dressed in pants, often with a man's belt, and she told Julia once that, if these young women continued to come by her office and use up her time, she'd put on some weight and learn to stutter.

Julia knew that Kate's mother was a teacher, maybe she still was, and her father was a mechanic. She had a younger brother who married and stayed in Bathurst; he and his wife had two daughters that Kate adored. After she finished Year 12 in Bathurst, she came to Canberra, where she finished a Bachelor's degree with honours in Psychology, English and American literature. She travelled to the University of Kansas at Lawrence to write her PhD on the use of time out with children in schools. She didn't want to live in the United States any longer than she had to, and applied for university positions back in Canberra.

They had been strong on behaviourism in Kansas; Skinnerian behaviour modification was certain to change the world. When she returned to Canberra, she was itching to break into schools and fix behaviours. Kate was dismayed when teachers smirked during her talks, or stood up and accused her of peddling bribery. Behaviourism in the classroom smacked of Room 101, or so they thought.

Kate fought criticism at first, then realised that, if she wanted converts, she had to change her words. When she asked teachers to help victims of violent behaviour, protect children from disappointment and help them become free-thinking, creative independent adults, she met less resistance. After Julia heard her speak at the main school over the way, she invited Kate to visit Wattle Street each week as an adviser, and fell in love with her.

Standing there using her best wind-down techniques, Kate tried to chase off the cow-eyed student, 'I have another meeting now,' she said. 'Maybe we can talk in class tomorrow.'

The nineteen-year-old turned her head, frowned at Julia, paused and said, 'Okay. Thanks, Kate. I'll look for that book, it sounds great.' She frowned again at Julia, waved bye-bye to Kate like a toddler, and walked down the hall.

Kate reached out her hand and Julia stepped past her into the gloom of her office. She left the door open.

'Coffee?'

'Thanks.'

She pulled a carton of milk from the short fridge in the corner and plugged in the electric kettle on the bookshelf. It grumbled and steam rose into the chilly room. Julia asked her about the Psychology staff meeting, but Kate looked down and didn't seem interested. She handed Julia a mug.

Leaning back in an easy chair, with a mug of coffee on her knee, she said, 'Your friend Ruth gave me a hard time this morning.'

Julia frowned. 'Yes.'

'Sunshine just follows her around.'

'Well…'

'What's her background?'

'She came out from Scotland, when she was about eighteen, I think, but she still has a spiky tongue.'

'Spiky? She can drop a woman at forty metres with her tongue.'

'Her husband's a bit wimpy, a school janitor. Tells her to stop cutting people off at the knees.'

'Or above the knees. The sound of her voice could cause impotence. Tell me they don't have any kids.'

'She does. Look, she makes a few enemies…'

'She yapped at me like a border collie this morning. I mean, her mouth has a mind of its own, but does she have a mind of her own?'

'She's good at her job. Most days I'm glad she's next door.' Julia sipped her coffee but it was too hot and she set it back down on the corner of Kate's desk.

'Seems like she hasn't been let out for a little while,' Kate said. 'Why can't she disagree without taking a sword to me?'

'She doesn't think you understand.'

Kate frowned. 'Her theories are dangerous.'

'Perhaps. But if this girl, Rose, has been interfered with, she couldn't be in better hands than Ruth's.'

'She couldn't be in better hands than yours.'

Julia looked away for a moment, a flush in her cheeks. 'I'm surprised to hear you complain about our meeting, given the meeting we just had.'

'The meeting we just had doesn't matter. It won't make a spot of difference to anyone outside that room.'

'What do you mean?'

'To understand fights in this department, you have to understand reprisal, and you have to go back six, seven, even ten years. They may look like they're arguing about principle, or today's space, or bricks, but they're exacting revenge for a past insult, forcing their rivals to surrender ground.'

'Ground?'

'Status. And rooms.'

Kate glanced at her watch. 'Anyway, I've got five minutes to prepare. Developmental psych today.'

'I'll go, then.'

'No, no, you don't have to go, not just yet. Let me look over these notes.' She squinted in the dim room, her green eyes shining. Shuffling notes on her lap, ordering them, she said, 'That should get me through an hour.' Then she looked up. 'I'll do it differently today, throw in some anthropology, maybe link it with some current thinking on families. Success of a lecture rests on its entertainment value, and how they, as nineteen or twenty-year-olds, can relate to your word pictures and your stories. Just new enough so it's interesting, just old enough so you don't threaten their values structure.'

Telling Julia how to master and win over youth.

Kate's room was a mess. Books of all colours and sizes along the walls, stacked on top of filing cabinets in no particular order, on her desk, in corners. In one corner lay the gym clothes she used to wind down each night. A dozen photographs of her brother's two children, Amy and Chris, sat in front of books on the shelves. In one, Chris stood in a green paddock holding a grey mare.

'Where was this taken?'

She was still in the substance of her lecture. 'On Jeff Mason's farm. Jeff was on sabbatical, so we stayed there.'

Julia held up a picture of Amy leading the same grey mare in a paddock. 'This was taken on the farm too?'

She looked back down at her notes. 'Yes.'

Julia wanted to ask more, but waited.

Five minutes later, Kate stood up and looked at herself in a small mirror she'd stuck to the inside of a wardrobe in the corner of the room. She squinted and brushed a hand over her black hair. 'Show time,' she said. 'Walk down with me.'

Julia lifted out of the deep chair. They left their cups on the desk, and walked out of her office into the cold gloomy hall of the Psychology department, down stairs leading to reception.

Kate smirked. 'This is the most erotic place in the university.'

Looking up the stairs to the reception desk, they gazed from underneath at a row of nubile young male and female bottoms as students leaned over the reception counter.

'Workmen love coming here,' she whispered, 'especially in summer when the women wear short skirts. They hang around on the lower floor, fix something, anything, even if it doesn't need fixing, and admire the view.'

Down the stairs and outside, Julia coasted along next to her as they rambled over nibbled grass.

Julia touched her arm. 'Can I ask you a favour?'

'Anything.'

'The Cavanaughs, the family of the girl coming into the unit, come from Bathurst. Your family, your parents and your brother come from Bathurst.'

'They're still in Bathurst. It's a small place.'

Can you ask them about Lee Cavanaugh?'

'I'll see what Mother knows.'

'Thanks.'

At the side door, Kate stopped and smiled, 'I'll see you then.'

'You will.' Julia felt coy and shy.

Two students tried to squeeze past her into the lecture hall.

Kate walked into the giant auditorium with two hundred undergraduates looking down from tiered rows. Most of them sat in the shadows up the back, leaving the front rows empty. She turned at the lecture podium and put her papers and overheads on the adjoining desk so she could slide them onto the projector in sequence and build to her crescendo. The show had to be slick. Out of her mouth came wisdom, absolute truth, or so she wanted them to believe.

Kate stood under the students' gaze, a low, growling murmur in the hall, then it went quiet. She reached up, scratched the bridge of her nose, cleared a strand of hair off one ear with her fingernail, and said, 'Today we'll explore some ideas from an anthropologist named van Gennup.' Her dark, smoky voice boomed into the back shadows.

Julia wanted to stay, but she stepped from the doorway, and walked down the path. She hoped the lecture went well.

7

Walk in the Forest

'God had an inordinate fondness for beetles.'

Taut as a violin string, Julia sat with little Ben, simmering and angry with herself, wishing he could speed up his story and get to the point.

'…and Jimmy started chucking things and the teacher put him on a chair.'

'Had to sit on a chair in the corner, did he?'

'No, by the teacher's desk.'

Did Ben resurrect these tedious stories about Jimmy because he thought his mother was a bad-boys expert, or because Jimmy was infamous?

As Brian came in, Claire sat drawing at the dining room table.

Ben looked up, 'Daddy,' and jumped off her lap.

Claire ran from the dining room. 'Look at the drawing I did of Mummy.'

He closed the door, set down his briefcase, and stared quietly at another crayon smudge of Mummy. 'It's good, darling.'

Julia looked down. 'Any mail?'

'Only bills.'

Brian staring down at her said, 'You going for your walk?'

Julia didn't look up. 'Yes, I need the air. I won't be long.'

She glanced at her watch – 4.15 – then looked down at Ben reading. She was struck by the feral restlessness that invaded her when Brian came home. Thinking for a moment of what limited her, and her lover. Kate's next-door neighbour was a teacher who knew Julia and

Brian; they shouldn't go to Kate's house, but sometimes they did and pretended it was a meeting.

She paced around the house once, then made another circuit, grabbed her coat out of the closet and said, 'It's still cold out,' and thought to herself, 'That's fairly obvious, isn't it?'

She stepped through the front door and hurried down the drive, patted Bonnie, and climbed into the Mazda. She started it with Claire, Ben and Brian watching from the living room window, backed out and travelled east along Redfern Street out of Cook through Aranda, down Caswell Drive and into another world.

Stepping out of the car, she climbed through the gate into red stringybark, white scribbly gum, wattle and the deep green of native cherry, over the border from suburbs. Stepping into wild ground.

Her pace was slow and easy. She set her feet where they wouldn't break any sticks or crunch any dried leaves, moving deliberately with no suddenness. Thirty metres in front of her a grey kangaroo with joey legs sticking out of its pouch jerked its head up and looked. Julia stopped and looked back, tense that she had stumbled onto the animal in long grass. The fine moment wasn't so much finding her, the fine moment came when the kangaroo twitched an ear, started to chew again, looking straight at Julia, then put down its head and nibbled grass. Cautiously, Julia moved slowly off to the side.

Further up the mountain, Julia heard the sudden clattering of white-plumed honeyeaters to the east, a hunting brown goshawk flying low through forest crown there. Sometimes they glimpsed him carrying slain birds up the hill.

A wind change from the south fluffed the back of her head, sending black hair whipping around the side of her face. A September storm was coming. A cold wind that could strip bark off the trees. To the west, a crag of pink cloud swelled and was cooked by low sun. The wet seemed to be some hours away and she and Kate would monitor colours in the sky and wouldn't be caught.

Julia rose to a secluded part of a steep gully halfway up the mountain, where a dark green pine tree stuck out from the bank. The tree stood against pastel grey scribbly gums. Cockatoos fed on hectares of cultivated pines to the south and flew into native bushland with pine cones. They seeded feral trees there. Park rangers carried pocketknives to ring-bark and kill them just as farmers had ring-barked the eucalypts two generations before. But this pine grew on safe ground on a part of the mountain that rangers never visited.

In the brown pine-needle nest under low boughs, Julia sheltered in the long skirt she'd worn during her full day of meetings. She glanced at her watch, closed her eyes in rest, and imagined Kate walking from her backyard, climbing over the fence into Aranda bushland. She would turn left through the forest, braking with her heels down the stony slope to the border of Caswell Drive, and cross into Black Mountain Reserve. As she jumped over the gully and climbed up Black Mountain, a gaggle of choughs, garrulous and squabbling, roamed through leaf litter ahead. She watched for people, looking behind her, over her shoulder, to her right and her left. There was no one else in the forest.

Julia opened her eyes and waited.

Kate approached through trees, eyes bright as she looked up. Julia sat with her knees under her chin as Kate moved up the hill towards her, smiling again, and reaching to Julia's outstretched hand.

Kate folded her knees and lay down. 'How much time do we have?'

'I have to be home at six.'

'But it's 4.45 now. Come on. Brian's home, he's perfectly capable of caring for them.'

'That's not the point.'

She looked to the west, dismayed by the low sun cradled in clouds.

Julia rested her head on Kate's neck and pushed into her arms. They lay back on the soft bed of grass and pine needles under the tree.

Hoarding the warmth of the winter sun, they lay for a time, then Julia turned and raised herself over Kate, looked down at dark lashes on her closed eyes and came down on her mouth.

She rolled off and laid her cheek on the grass, looked into her face. 'I love you.'

Kate opened her eyes.

'Come on,' said Julia, 'let's walk further up the hill.' She rolled onto her stomach, and pushed to her feet. Julia glanced at the smoothness of her arms.

They turned and hiked further up the hill, Kate following through a maze of brittle gums.

It was always hard to write in her diary about the drunkenness of losing control, and her diary was baggy with platitudes, and Julia didn't care. If they hadn't seen each other for two days, they would glance at each other in a room full of people and shake, unable to maintain a conversation with anyone else. They nurtured loss of control, grew it like hothouse tomatoes. They commiserated about people who couldn't swerve out of control.

Black Mountain was their territory and they hunted over it, wanted to drive back anyone who roamed over their ground. Hiking over the hill, they reached the next gully, this one more isolated and further from walking trails than the pine. Lacy wattles and delicate hakeas led to a native cherry tree shaped like a fat teardrop, or a green dome in the Kremlin, or an onion. The tree gave them refuge from rain and sun, a roof, a shield from people's gaze. They crouched low and slipped under sloping boughs, a latticework of limbs over them. As Kate curled into their lair, Julia knelt, sliding her fingers up her leg. A warm soft hand inside her thigh gliding up with spread fingers.

'I'm glad you don't understand how beautiful you are,' she said, and reached up under her blouse.

They lay with Julia's jacket under them.

They made love for a time, neither of them knew how long. They whispered and saw visions and cried out. They lay still with the air quiet around them, breathing onto each other's skin. A drowsiness fell over them, like mist through the tree.

Slowly the chattering of small birds and brushing wind in the forest stirred them. Julia watched Kate's face as she slept and felt wide awake and powerful. The sun pierced through limbs and moved patterns of branches over her sleeping face.

Kate opened her eyes, blinked for a moment, and looked at her lover. 'Promise you won't go away from me.'

'I won't.'

'You've given your word.'

'I've given my word. Now, don't feel slighted if I ask you what time it is.'

'Six.'

'What! We've been here an hour! Come on!'

Julia crouched low and moved sideways, like a land crab out from under the native cherry. Kate followed.

'Let's go.'

They burst, half-running, half-walking down the ridge, out of the gully, down a rocky hill towards Caswell Drive. Into low sun with hands shading their brows they rushed, arms slapping twigs and branches in front of them.

Kate knew Julia was worried about her family, so she talked about work, and panted, and shifted her focus. 'When's Rose Cavanaugh coming in?'

Half-panting, Julia said, 'Tomorrow.' Stepping down the rocky hill.

They hurtled down Black Mountain, brushing tea-tree from their faces with arms in front of their eyes, leaping over wandering vines of hardenbergia, a trickling creek with Julia's skirt flying up. Kate followed.

They pushed to the edge of dusk, bloody clouds lay on mountains to the west. They knew there would be no storm. Near the road, Julia grew unsettled, eyes darting left and right, over her shoulder, watching for people.

'No one around,' said Kate.

'Who cares anyway?'

'It hurts to be away from you.'

'Yes. I wish we didn't have to meet this way.'

'Can I phone you?'

'At work, but not at home. Brian's suspicious. You can hardly blame him.'

'I'll see you next Thursday.'

'Don't forget. You promised to find out about the Cavanaughs in Bathurst, especially Lee.'

'I will.'

Julia slid her arm over Kate's shoulder, pulled her body close, and kissed the side of her mouth. 'Don't forget how much I love you.' She smelled strong, like fine sweet wood. Julia's hand slid down her arm, through her fingers.

Kate stood with her hands in her pockets and watched her jog along the dirt track to her car. As Julia reached her Mazda and pulled keys from her pocket, Kate turned and loped across Caswell Drive to her house on the hill.

8

New Girl

Homosexuality is easy to explain using
biology. Religion is harder.

The golden promise of a sunny day unfolded through trees in the
street. All the sadness of the city lifted. Faces crowded in misty bus
windows and children left their houses for school.

Ruth shook her head and sucked in her lips. 'Rose told a neighbour
and the neighbours told the cops. Now she denies it. Seen that a few
times, haven't we? Stepdad fiddles with the stepdaughter, stepdaughter
lies to police to protect the stepdad. Nobody goes to jail.'

'So you think it's true,' said Julia.

Ruth started to flick her middle finger against the nails on her left
hand, 'Don't you?'

'Let's wait and see. You're often right about these things.'

'Of course I'm right. We'll get something out of them in this first
interview.'

'Something out of them? When they're sworn to secrecy? What do
we get, shifty eyes?'

Her mouth set hard. 'Let's just see what he's like.'

She turned to leave but there were shambling steps along the
hallway and Jeremy scuffed in through the open doorway holding a
tangle of papers under one arm.

'Morning. Cavanaughs today?'

'Just talking about it,' said Ruth. 'What else do you have on them?'

'Only what I've said. Welfare asked us to keep our eyes open. It
seems that…' He broke off and looked at the door. 'They're here.'

Ruth hopped off Julia's desk and stood with them; three wordless people standing together.

Bob walked in, blocking the light from the door, wrinkles under his smiling eyes, 'Morning, everyone, morning. You three hatching a plot, are you?'

A smaller man followed who they knew must be Lee Cavanaugh, about thirty-five, lean, with light brown hair combed from low down one side up over the top of his balding head. He had the start of a pot belly poking through buttons in his striped brown shirt. He was scruffy, as if he didn't care about shaving or bathing or fashion, and spent no time in front of the mirror except to work on his vanishing hair.

Julia's attention started to wander. She couldn't stop her father's advice about men with comb-overs booming into her head; her father had no regard for timing and he didn't that morning. She stood facing Lee Cavanaugh determined to be fair and impartial, but already she disliked him.

Following Lee, in short tentative steps, came a small stooped woman with purple bags under her eyes, pallid skin, oily brown hair, in a simple print dress. Rose's mother Holly and, clearly, the world had defeated her. Perhaps Lee had defeated her. She looked too old to have two young children, Rose's sisters were only two and four according to the file, but it was easy to see in her expression and in her stature that living was hard, a mouth that creased down at the corners, a forehead hatched by horizontal lines cut by vertical stripes over her nose. Given some hope, she would have looked under thirty, but she harboured no hope that morning and looked more than fifty.

Last in the parade, lugging her feet into the room with her head down, a scrawny flat-chested girl with honey-coloured hair and a face as smooth as a river stone. She had blue shadows under her eyes and looked younger than twelve. She had the opportunity for beauty in the bones of her face, like a painting out of Vermeer that could grow into a lovely angular face with wide-set eyes. But she was skinny as a spider and angry, and she made her eyes narrow and tight. Julia thought she would grow up ugly.

Bob and the Cavanaugh family stopped in front of them, Lee and Bob standing side by side, and Rose and her mother lurking behind them.

Bob hoisted up his pants and started introductions. As usual, he was clumsy and too loud, but somehow honest. His voice made the classroom feel like an RSL club. 'Lee and Holly Cavanaugh, and Rose, I'd like you to meet Ruth McGill, she takes the older kids, and Julia Honeychurch, she'll be your teacher, and Jeremy Gatewood, he's our school psychologist.'

Ruth stretched out a hand, leaned forward so Lee had to shake it and look straight into her eyes. 'Nice to meet you, Lee. I hope we can work together.'

Julia was imagining his hand limp and moist. He looked unsettled as he tried to hold Ruth's hard stare. He widened his mouth to a smile, but the smile was short and false. On the outside, he acted like the calm settled man, but inside he was frightened.

Lee's eyes darted away, just slightly as Ruth let go of his hand. 'Yeah,' he replied, 'nice to meet you. We sure want to get her straightened out.' Lee turned and looked at Jeremy, again trying to smile, but the rest of his face wouldn't cooperate. 'We know Jeremy because of the tests and things he did. We reckon that's a good start in finding out what's wrong with her.' Then he turned to Julia, holding the frozen smile. 'Good to meet you, Julia,' and he reached over to shake her hand. Lee seemed to learn quickly how things were done.

Rose stood behind her mother Holly, and Holly behind Lee, a sullen, uncertain row of Cavanaughs. Mother and daughter looked down, seeming to study their feet.

Ruth touched her shoulder again, 'Thanks for coming in, Holly,' and Holly responded with a limp, embarrassed hand, grasped in the certainty of Ruth's powerful fingers. 'And you too, Rose.' She reached to Rose but the girl held tightened fists to her sides like she wanted to hide dirt under her nails.

'I have to get back to the main school,' said Bob. 'Leave you to it. Good luck, Rose. Glad you're with us.' He wheeled around in size twelve shoes and rushed out.

'With us?' Julia thought. 'You'll never see them again.'

Ruth laid her hand on Rose's arm. 'I'll explain some of the rules, so everything's clear.'

'Go ahead,' said Lee. 'She has to understand this is her last chance.'

Holly was clutching her throat in a sign of privation and offering no backing to the actors in the little performance.

'There's a rule about violence. If you have a tantrum, rip anything off the wall, hit people, your parents take you home, or we send you home on the bus. Your parents return with you next morning to renegotiate your place in the unit. Any problems with that?' Ruth looked in turn at Lee, then at Holly, who was looking away, and then at young Rose, who was still looking down.

'That's fine,' said Lee.

Ruth explained the other rules, about smoking, school boundaries, and the home note. Lee acted the semi-gentleman.

After ten minutes, she had finished, and it was impossible to determine how much Lee, Holly and Rose had taken in.

Ruth said, 'Nice to meet you. See you later, then.' She walked out and they could hear rubber-soled shoes marching down the hall.

Jeremy stood without speaking, and Julia waited for Lee and Holly to catch up and meet her eyes.

Julia said, 'I'm sure Rose and I will get along fine.'

Holly gave one of those wolf-pup smiles, head tipped to the side, a pained, forcing up of the corners of her mouth like she would roll over and let someone lick her belly.

'Okay,' said Lee. He smiled and placed his hand on Rose's shoulder. 'We'll leave you to it.'

Julia disliked the way Lee assumed a casual, home boy manner with her. When he smiled and laid his hand on Rose's shoulder, Rose pulled away and ducked under his touch. Holly lifted her eyes just off the floor and watched her daughter walk to the back of the classroom. At the time, Julia thought it was an odd show of independence for a troubled child in a strange place.

Lee said, 'Goodbye then, kid.'

Rose kept her back to him.

'Well, Holly, Lee,' said Julia, 'we look forward to seeing you again.' As it came out, she knew it tasted like a lie, but it was a necessary lie in the righteous cause of saving a broken child, or some such nonsense.

As the children worked at their desks, red-headed Peter Clark glanced over his shoulder at Jason, smirking, disobedient with mock, sleepy eyelids. He glanced back at Rose, and nodded towards her for Jason to see. The two boys had been skulking all morning, saying little, not sure how to act in front of the new girl. By 11.30, they wanted some excitement. Jason raised his hand and asked Julia if he could go to the toilet. Julia said yes, and he stood and left. Five minutes later, as he entered the room, he brushed hard against Peter sitting at his desk.

Peter would normally scream about the brutality of an institution that penalised him yesterday for doing the same thing but allowed this troublemaker to run free today. Where was the justice? Where was the fair play? Where was the leadership? But not today. He giggled.

No one had the courage to walk by and brush up against the new girl. But Peter would. He had an older sister and could teach the others about girl psychology. Up from his desk, over to the pencil sharpener, grinding his pencil for too long, then back to his seat and – bang, on the back of Rose's head with his elbow.

'You little bastard.' Rose's first words that day, loud and pent-up. 'Fucking dickhead,' and she leapt from her desk, glowered and wheeled towards him with her fist raised.

Calmly Julia said, 'Rose, just leave him to me.'

'No,' she yelled. 'Fuck you.' With her eyebrows low, she reached over to the chart on the wall, ripped it down with tacks clattering on the floor. She rushed at Peter.

'Rose, I'll deal with it.' Julia shouted, and Peter ducked low in his desk, pulled his head in like a turtle.

'If you fight in this room, or wreck things, you'll have to go home.' Julia was pleading, and she knew it was a mistake.

'Fuck you!' shouted Rose.

'I'm asking you, please.'

'Are you deaf?' she bellowed.

Rose darted to her desk, picked up her chair and threw it across the room at Peter, but it fell short, banging and clattering as it rolled into the corner.

'Jason, would you please get Mrs McGill for me?'

He stood and rushed out of the room and was back in thirty seconds with Ruth.

'Rose, can you come with me please?' said Julia.

No response. Rose squatted on the floor and tucked her face into her knees.

In sulk mode now, Julia thought the storm had passed. 'Rose, you understand that I have to phone your parents now.'

Wordless, her face hidden in her knees.

Julia looked at Ruth. 'You okay for a minute?'

'Fine.'

Julia walked into Jeremy's office. He looked up. 'We have a tantrum.'

'We do.'

Suddenly, from the classroom came a mournful sobbing. 'Don't send me home. Please, don't send me home. He'll kill me.'

Julia looked at Jeremy. 'What do we do? What if she's telling the truth?'

'What if she's telling a story?'

Rose wailed in the next room, 'Don't send me home.'

Her cries followed Julia around the office as she paced from one wall to the other.

Jeremy said. 'Boys set her up, didn't they?'

'Wasn't too hard.'

'And you know what all that wailing is about.'

'Who's on my side? I know. Who's on my side against Lee? But what do we do?'

'She wants us to kidnap her.'

Julia listened to Rose wailing next door. 'Not now, Jeremy. What do we do?'

'That wailing is what she did at her old school. She bleated and cried, "Don't tell my dad, he'll kill me," and the teachers didn't tell Lee and she got more violent, and still she bleated, "Don't tell my dad," and they didn't tell him, then Rose started hitting kids, and teachers, and anyone who crossed her path. Setting fires. Eventually she was expelled. She plays one adult against the other and, the better it works, the more she plays up.'

'Look, there is some basis for these stories about Lee. Come on, you've met him. He's a creep.'

'He supposedly beats her at night. We don't know that he'll beat her over this. Welfare is supposed to protect her. We inform them if we suspect anything.'

'You're callous for a vegetarian. But, of course, Adolf was a vegetarian, wasn't he?' Julia glanced down at the Tupperware container full of sprouts and dried tomatoes on Jeremy's desk.

'She has to go home,' he said.

'Tell me,' said Julia, 'does Lee Cavanaugh know that welfare is watching him?'

'Probably. Yes, I think so.'

'Even if there's a chance of abuse, we send her home.'

'The chance of abuse is there whether we send her home, or she walks home after school, or her mother goes into hospital to have another baby.'

Julia shook her head, 'Why isn't $60,000-a-year Bob making this decision?'

'$60,000-a-year Bob wouldn't have the foggiest idea what to do.

Bob has nothing to recommend him for this job, except maybe his shoe size.'

'Anyway,' Julia gazed out the window at light wind flexing and arcing the wrists on eucalypt branches, 'you have the Cavanaughs' number?'

'Yes, in here.' Jeremy shuffled through paper in one of his expandable files. 'Just hang on, I'll find it.'

Rose wailed next door.

'Jeremy, you'd be more organised if you had a good feed of red meat once a week.'

Julia stepped out the door and looked in her classroom. Rose slumped against the wall, dead still. Julia stepped back into Jeremy's room.

More shuffling. 'Right. Here it is,' grasped in his hand was the file with CAVANAUGH printed in tall red letters on the edge.

Julia opened it, and pulled out the admission form.

The number rang twice, it kept ringing, it rang ten times.

'Nobody's home.'

Then the click as the receiver was picked up. The gruff, groggy voice of Lee, just woken from sleep, or maybe drunk. 'Hello.'

'Lee?'

'Who's this?'

'Julia Honeychurch, from Rose's school.'

'Oh yeah. What's happened?'

'Sorry to have to phone you on Rose's first morning, but she's had a bit of a turn.'

'A fight?'

'Not exactly. She lost her temper.'

'Doesn't surprise me.'

'Yes, well, she knows she has to go home.'

'You want me to come and get her?'

'If you could.'

'Has to be done, doesn't it?'

'Normal procedure.'

Silence at Lee's end.

'Uh, Lee, I need to mention a couple things. Firstly, she's quite upset, crying, pleading with us, asking us not to send her home because, she says, you'll beat her.'

'Beat her?'

'Yes, beat her. And I've given her my assurance, given her my word that you won't beat her.'

Silence at Lee's end of the phone.

Jeremy looked up at Julia. Julia frowned back and shook her head.

'What I didn't say to her, and this is the second thing, Welfare spoke to us, and they want us to report any problems with Rose.'

Still quiet at Lee's end of the line.

'We're keen to work with you and Holly, and we don't like Welfare meddling in our school.'

No sound at the other end of the phone.

'Lee?'

'Yeah. I'm here.'

'You can understand our problem.'

'You've got a problem all right.'

'Lee, I've guaranteed her that nothing will happen to her.'

'Yeah,' Lee's voice subdued.

Julia couldn't tell whether he was angry, or bored, or thinking. 'Good. Thanks, Lee. We'll see you soon.'

Jeremy watched her hang up the phone. 'Well done,' he said.

'We'll see if he beats her. If he doesn't, then I suppose it was well done.'

'We have little choice. Spread the guilt thinly.'

Julia walked back to the classroom and the wailing Rose.

Lee arrived in fifteen minutes. They heard his rubber boots squeak down the hallway, past the toilets. As he came closer, Rose stood from the floor, moved to the furthest corner of the classroom and crouched.

Jeremy intercepted Lee in the hallway and said, 'Julia wants to see you. I'll take her class.'

They met in Jeremy's office and she said, 'Thanks for coming.'

'Yeah, fine.' He smiled and stared as if the power of hatred in his open blue eyes would carry the day.

She wanted to slap the helpful stepfather. She buried what she felt and was calm and said, 'I promised her she wouldn't be hit when she leaves today.'

Lee rubbed the back of his neck, petted his hair, like a master and dog in one. With a stained oily hand, he brushed aside the suggestion. 'Yeah, yeah, fine. It's fine. She'll be fine.'

He strolled into the classroom towards Rose as Jeremy and the boys watched her cower. Lee reached down to take her upper arm; he pulled her to her feet. Rose yanked back, jerked her arm away and sank to the floor. Julia was thinking that Rose would rather handle snakes than be touched by Lee. Lee reached down, grabbed her arm again, squeezed, and pulled up on the dead weight lifting Rose to her feet. She relented, sank against the wall. He lifted her by one arm. A mask stared back as she allowed him to push her out of the room with his dirty hand tight on her upper arm.

'Can we meet tomorrow morning,' Julia asked, 'and start afresh?'

Rose was stony-faced, looking straight ahead.

'We'll be here,' said Lee.

'It would be best if you and Holly met with us once a fortnight. Can we do that?'

He shrugged. 'We'll see.' He didn't bother with the forced smile, and Julia understood that meant 'no'.

'See you tomorrow, Rose,' Julia said.

She ignored Julia, and Julia followed her out, watched Lee push her down the hall and out to the parking lot.

She followed them to Lee's grimy white plumber's van. Rose allowed herself to be pushed into the back like a criminal. She looked straight ahead, but her hatred was directed at Julia.

They left and Julia watched. She turned to the school and met her own eyes reflected in the classroom window, the eyes of a traitor. She looked away.

9

Simple Lessons

'There are three things which are too wonderful for me, yes,
four which I do not understand: the way of an eagle in the
air, the way of a serpent on a rock, the way of a ship in the
midst of the sea, and the way of a man with a virgin.'

Julia wept during the night and she didn't know for whom. By 3 a.m.,
she was ready for the knock on the door. She got up, pulled on her
robe, opened the front door and the woman stood on the porch in a
Marlowe sort of trench coat with a single loose knot at the waist.

The woman's hair was yellow, in a pageboy cut looped under a
fedora. In pale moonlight, she held a clipboard. 'Ms Honeychurch?'

'Yes.'

'Julia Honeychurch?'

'What do you want at this hour?'

'Ms Honeychurch, I need just a minute of your time.'

'What's this about?'

'We've been watching you.'

'What?'

'Watching you.'

'You have?'

'I'm afraid so, Ms Honeychurch. We have. So you know why I'm
here.'

'No, I don't.'

'It's obvious, Ms. Honeychurch.'

'What's obvious?'

'The enormity of your offences.'

'They can't be. Are they?'

'I'm afraid so.'

Julia paused for a moment. 'How long did it take you to find out?'

'Not long. It was clear from the first day we started watching you.'

Julia looked away.

'Anyway, Ms Honeychurch, let's get this over with. I've come to inform you that we've known for some time now that you have no idea what you're doing. Quite a few people have been fooled, you've put on a brave face, you've been resolute in the face of conflict, sort of a fake confidence really, and you should be congratulated for that. But you didn't fool us.'

'It's sort of a relief in a way. Who else knows?'

'The kids at Wattle Street know, that little homeland for the bewildered and lost, and some of their parents know too. That's not surprising. Didn't you notice how they smirked? I mean, after all, your own family's no model to follow, is it?'

'Did I fool the people I work with?'

'Not really. Now Jeremy, he's a nice man, isn't he? A real haircut. A bad dresser, oh dear, so last season, and he worries too much. But he's a nice fellow and you've managed to fool him. Keep up the pretence with Jeremy.'

'But you know.'

'Oh yes, we know.'

Julia nodded. 'Well, thank you for coming.'

'I won't say "my pleasure", Ms Honeychurch, but someone had to tell you.'

'Thank you. Watch the hose over the path.'

'Thank you, I will.' She stalked into the night.

As the night hardened with cold, Julia dozed. Brian lay asleep and she'd wake him if she stirred. But she couldn't stay. She stepped onto bare floorboards in the quiet room, padded around the house and looked out the window at white eucalypts standing in ground mist under a thin moon. She started to think about beginnings for some reason, as if early successes and failures and delusions had built some clear narrative wisdom. Often at night, she travelled to the desert on a black horse under a red moon to visit Marlene.

Ten years ago, Marlene had lived in a shed with no plumbing on the Mission, a collection of corrugated iron huts that sheltered in ochre sandhills north of Port Augusta, that sweet hopeless little town in the north. On a Saturday morning, Julia drove out from Port Augusta along a dirt track with dust boiling out from under her Holden. She stopped at Marlene's little house. Skinny dogs sniffed at garbage blown against the outside wall and a woman in a knitted cap and dirty black T-shirt washed herself at an outdoor tap.

Julia knocked and found Marlene's father at home.

With two days of silver stubble on his face, he stood in the doorway, smiled and nodded, then looked back into the house, 'Marlene. Marlene, your teacher.' With some wariness, he waved Julia into the cooking smells and spare furnishings of his sitting room.

Marlene stood in the middle of the room with her eyes cast down.

He asked Julia to sit at the table in dim light, fired up the gas burner, and they drank tea from the family's stained porcelain cups. Julia saw herself as a saviour, an idealist, sensitive to the disadvantaged. She knew that the greatest humiliation for Marlene would be if she, Julia, came to advise her father, talked down to him in front of Marlene, like he was a child himself. So Julia talked very little at first. She listened and tried to win his trust, tried to be one of the poor. Like most young people, she was stupid and blind to the humiliation she caused, inept at doing good deeds.

He was patient with her. After ten minutes or so, a scrap of mistrust fell away from his face and he opened up. He warmed a little and told her about trips up north to visit relatives, wild ostriches near the Mission, a failed attempt to farm them at the turn of the century. Julia had seen their broad plumes floating over hot sand into Mulga trees.

Marlene, in a flowered print dress, an old white cardigan and high-topped basketball shoes that cost her father too much, slouched in a chair. The shoes were a fashionable badge. On the first day she had them, Marlene showed everybody at school. Marlene and her friends were consummate basketball players with long sticky fingers and stick legs that gave them an advantage over white girls in the region. They beat white girls badly in these contests.

While Julia talked to her father, Marlene sat and drew coloured-pencil sketches of red sandhills and green mulga trees scattered over them. She hunched over the rough kitchen table drawing white eucalypts in long lines filing out of the Flinders Ranges, and emus and blue-tongued lizards and forms that Julia didn't recognise.

In the following week, she started to take Julia for walks. They sauntered through sand hills like sisters, bumping shoulders and saying little. Port Lincoln parrots and budgerigars, splashed emerald and yellow over their heads and down through red gums along Spear Creek. After rain, the hot, still days smelled like cough medicine from the eucalypts and salt air coming off Spencer's Gulf. Red kangaroos with tight muscled arms rose from sandy beds in blue-bush. The males stretched high, stared and menaced Julia and Marlene before springing in arcs down the creek. During some walks a black falcon drifted over, silent and high, using the two women as beaters in long grass. They flushed stubble quail and crested pigeons, and the falcon stooped and snared them in her long grey toes.

Things were going well. But three weeks after they started their walks, Marlene refused to come. In class, she sat withdrawn and crushed, divided from the others. A few days later, she turned crazy. At the time, Julia didn't take it personally; she knew the demons that came with adolescence. Marlene started to bicker with teachers and Julia, and clash with her friends. The school girls talked endlessly about Marlene.

Travelling on the yellow school bus one morning, she roamed up and down the aisle, cursed old friends, moaned about betrayal, kicked girls and seized their hair. The school asked a GP to see her, and the GP wrote a letter to a psychiatrist who travelled to Port Augusta once a month. The psychiatrist smiled at Marlene and greeted her father with the sort of genial condescension that doctors use in place of warmth. He recommended Valium, and a life of quiet for one week; Marlene didn't seize any of her wary friends by the hair and slam their faces into the ground. She slouched against the brick wall in the schoolyard and didn't talk to any girls. She wouldn't talk to Julia. Marlene stared at her own feet, even smirked to mock Julia if Julia asked how she was and talked into the crown of Marlene's bowed head.

In the following week, she turned into a mad creature, warlike and snarling and treacherous. She bellowed at her friends, tossed them down stairs, beat them into the concrete, and screamed like a banshee. A crouching demon burst from inside Marlene and snarled and slapped at them, and crept back inside her to wait for the next opportunity.

That next day, Marlene failed to trap one of her friends against the brick wall on the playground, so she rushed inside to the empty classroom, grabbed her enemy's chair, and crashed it with force through the high window out onto the concrete.

Then she vanished. One friend told Julia that she'd left school, but another said she'd been sick. Julia visited Marlene's father like she had that first Saturday morning and tried to uncover her secret. Her father stood in dim light, confused and mute. Julia questioned him, and inadvertently displayed suspicion when he didn't reply, so it was no surprise that he shut down, looked at the floor and sealed the mystery away from her. There was a long difficult silence before Julia turned and left. But people at the Mission told Marlene's friends and these friends told Julia that Marlene had gone up north to stay with an uncle.

'Why?' she asked.

'We don't know.' They looked away and it hurt Julia that they lied so easily.

A month later, she sat planning the morning's lesson when a dark form drifted in beside her, touched her arm. She looked up. 'Marlene.'

She looked happier and smiled as if they hadn't been enemies after all.

Julia complimented her on her new print dress and high-topped shoes and didn't ask where she'd been. 'When can we start our walks again?'

Marlene stood next to the desk and shrugged. Julia picked up a pen and started to write, and Marlene handed her a brown exercise book. She forced it between Julia and her work. Diagonally, in coloured print from the upper left-hand corner down to the lower right she had written 'Aboriginal Life'.

Julia opened the book and Marlene stood looking away.

'Thank you.'

She turned and drifted out the door.

Late that night, Julia had time to look over Marlene's book. She had titled the inside front cover 'Our Life' and had neatly coloured each page with drawings of blue hills and grey gorges, river red gums, coolabah trees, a galah, an eagle and things important to her. Each chapter discussed dancing, birds or the like, and some of the text was copied directly from some dry source that Julia doubted Marlene could read – 'The form of initiation varied in different regions, with circumcision being an important part of it…'

But she had written parts of it in limited English, perhaps with some friend. '…they have a law that if you live with aboriginal man you must not filthy word at the man or the woman can geted boned.' On the following page was a story: 'Once upon a time a girl name Marlene she got boned and she did not now that she was bone. She went to the hospital to see the doctor. But that doctor said that he could not help her. So she went to Oodnadatta to see her uncle and she had got better at last she was better again. Before when I had gone to the mission I see her standing near her father. I said Marlene come with us but she was mad and silly in the head.'

Julia kept the book with her that night but couldn't grasp what it meant. The book left Julia troubled and uneasy. In the early dark, she woke on twisted sheets, switched on the light and tried to read it again.

At school the next day, she asked one of Marlene's friends to explain the story. Her friend laughed and walked away.

'Please,' said Julia.

The friend turned and came back. She stood quietly for a moment before she told her that Marlene had travelled north to see her uncle. He spoke to Raven, their totem, for advice about Marlene's sickness. Her uncle had learned that Marlene's mother had violated tribal law, used bad language with Marlene's father, and, worse, she had probably slept with another man. Late one night a Kadaicha man came in from the north, feathers covering his feet so he left no tracks in the red Port Augusta sand. He pointed the bone at Marlene's mother to punish her wrongdoing, but missed her mother, and embedded the bone in Marlene's breast. Her mother escaped the penalty she deserved, but Marlene didn't.

After Marlene's uncle removed the bone from her breast, she stayed with him for two weeks before returning to Port Augusta. As Julia recalled, sitting now in her Canberra house with the rest of her family asleep, Marlene found some happiness there, or at least as much happiness as a young Aboriginal girl in that dusty divided town was entitled to.

Ten years later, Julia stepped onto a chair in her sitting room, squinted along the top shelf and found the notebook. A hole was torn in the plastic cover, and it was stained and one corner lay creased into the pages. She laid it on top of her briefcase.

10

Phone Call

> 'And not many days after, the younger son gathered all
> together and took his journey into a far country, and
> there wasted his substance with riotous living.'

That morning, Lee and Holly failed to bring Rose to school.

When Julia phoned the house, Lee answered.

'She's sick.' He offered nothing more, as if to say, 'Your move, teacher.'

'Thanks, Lee. We look forward to seeing you tomorrow.'

'Yeah. Sure.' Lee hung up.

Julia turned from the phone. 'Why do we bother?'

'We're crippled with "rescue complex",' said Jeremy. 'Probably in the DSM III.'

'Our friends were smart enough to rise like shooting stars in the public service, buy sailing boats and new cars, fly to London or Bali, and we study behaviour modification and stay back with the losers. A little homeland for the bewildered.'

'Who calls Wattle Street a homeland for the bewildered?'

'The same people who call it a George Orwell theme park,' she said. 'The police and other teachers snigger behind our backs. You know they do.'

Jeremy was quiet for a time before he said, 'You're talking about Rose, and about Lee.'

Julia looked down and continued to mark papers. 'Who knows what I'm talking about? He's a contemptible insect. If she's covered in bruises, he won't send her in.'

Julia sat on the lounge with Claire on her lap, listening to her read.

The phone next to the couch rang and Claire reached over and answered it. 'Hello, Claire Honeychurch speaking. Uh-huh. Yes, she's here.' She looked up and handed over the phone. 'Mummy, it's for you.'

'Hello.'

Claire stayed on her lap, quietly mumbling words.

'Hi, darling,' said Kate, 'I just wanted to thank you for the lovely time on Black Mountain.'

'Um…yes, okay.'

'Making myself clear, am I?'

'You're into the Chardonnay tonight.'

'Am I?'

'Or something.'

'Does it show?'

'It shows. What can I do for you tonight?'

'Just what you're doing now. Talk to me. Have some fun. Anyone there?'

'Yes, Claire's here.'

'You don't want to talk about Black Mountain.'

'Not now.'

'You want to talk about work.'

'There's no choice.' Julia didn't know whether Claire heard Kate's voice through the receiver.

'Okay, boring work.'

'I can talk about Rose. She's come in, we met her mum and dad. Well, her stepdad really.'

'And?'

'Well, things started out like Ruth said they would – the boys posed and showed off to each other all day. But it wasn't one of the boys who blew up. Rose blew up. We had to send her home.'

'Why?'

'You have to come down hard from the beginning, or you lose them. Engage parents, like it or not. It was a hard lesson for us to learn when we started, but we learned it and now it's policy.'

'On her first day?'

'Not unusual. They don't believe us until we do it. But it worried us to send her home, to Lee. Now she hates me.'

'What did Ruth and Jeremy say?'

'I didn't have time to discuss it with Ruth. She took the kids for me. But I talked it over with Jeremy, and he said Rose had to go home.'

'These vegetarians are a puzzle, aren't they?'

'Yes.'

'I thought Jeremy would sit with Rose for an hour and listen to whale songs.'

'Are you interested in this or not?'

'You know I am.'

'I talked to Lee before he came to get her, sort of warned him that Welfare wanted us to report any abuse. He seemed to hear me. Rose didn't respond to any of us in the unit, and she recoils from Lee. She didn't come in today, and Lee said he'd bring her in tomorrow. Any ideas about getting through to her?'

Claire shifted on Julia's lap, her tiny weight gave some comfort, but Julia was tense about Brian. A car passed in the street.

Kate was quiet on the other end of the line. Finally she said, 'I don't want to sidestep your question, but I need more facts. If Lee interfered with her, or anyone did, she won't trust adults, and that includes you.'

'We think she's been interfered with, but there's not too much we can do about it. We need strategies now. We need to try something tomorrow before we lose her.'

'I still don't like prescribing strategies for a child I haven't seen, drunk over the phone.'

'Make a suggestion. Let me decide if it's appropriate or not.'

Kate was quiet, and then said, 'You're a fine girl, and you deserve my guidance.'

'I deserve more than that.'

'Sorry, can't think of a thing.'

'Then I will. Animals. I had a girl in Port Augusta once, not unlike

Rose, except for bony dogs lapping gutter water outside her shack. She did a project that I'll show to Rose, if Rose ever comes back. We'll organise an orphaned joey, or a possum or something she can watch over and build trust with. Help her with the animal, relate to her through the animal, talk about the problems she faces with the animal, and talk about progress. Then build the experience into a metaphor, a story about herself.'

'Jeremy should come at that.'

'He will.'

'Working with the animal won't help Rose. Sorry, it just doesn't work that way. But if she can see herself grow or heal as the animal grows and heals, up to the point where the animal is ready to go back, you could have a little ceremony, and that ceremony could mark an emerging new Rose, help establish a bond between you and her.'

'Pretty new-age for a cynic like you.'

Claire looked up.

'Or you can try whale songs,' said Kate.

'Secretly, I mean, out of the closet, you're pretty traditional, aren't you?'

'Absolutely,' said Kate. 'I tell my students to forget about choice and put their future in the hands of God.'

'No you don't.'

'Okay, so I don't. Use the strengths of the people in Wattle Street.'

'It doesn't take a Nobel laureate to work that out,' said Julia.

'Forget about Bob. If Bob won a trip to Paris for two, he'd go twice. But Jeremy could work with this.'

'Did you learn anything about Lee from your friends or family in Bathurst?'

'I learned a little bit. He's a fake like the rest of us.'

'Riddles again.'

'My mother taught with Lee's mother in Bathurst. I spoke to her last night. She knows Lee.'

'And?'

'Trouble as a kid.'

'Trouble?'

'Yes, and his parents still live there.'

'In Bathurst?'

'Yes.'

'Do his parents see Lee and Holly now?'

'I don't think so. Lee's father, John, was a school inspector in the New South Wales school system, and there was some family money. They're well off and respected in Bathurst. His father is a hard man, organised, with perfect grammar, puts on a white shirt and tie if he walks down the street for a newspaper. Successful. As I said, Lee's mother's a teacher.'

Julia had a flash of Lee in his oily shirt and jeans smelling like sewage, dirt under his nails standing in his parents' home while his father pointed to his own sock drawer, as neat as a crate of eggs and said, 'Like this.' Screaming now, 'Like this or you don't go out tonight.'

'Did Lee hate school?'

'I don't think it was quite that simple. Lee was bright, did well in school, dux of his class in Year 10, chess club, sports hero in the newspapers. As shiny clean as they come.

'But he's a bogan.'

'Back then, he did everything his father asked him to do. But his father wouldn't even grudgingly give approval for his excellence. Sour bastard, he is, hard and sour about something. When Lee was about sixteen, he started to misbehave a little, as sixteen-year-olds do. His parents had only experienced a smiling, perfectly behaved little boy who loved books. So they fought him, they didn't ride it out like a lot of parents do. John decided to beat the rebelliousness out of his son, break him down. They grounded him for weeks on end.'

'What did the school do?'

'No idea. Anyway, things got worse. His father tried to regain control, and Lee fought him. His mother lay stranded between them. Finally, the police caught Lee smoking marijuana in the park with some kids. John went through the roof. Lee had delivered public humiliation to the Cavanaugh household, something the family couldn't stomach. There was a terrible fight that night, Lee and John shrieking at each other, John getting thunderous and more violent. He could be a vicious character. Lee's mother tried to intervene, but Lee shouted something like "I never want to end up like you!" at his father, and John responded, apparently without thinking, "Don't worry, you never will. You're not mine anyway."'

'Not mine anyway?"

Kate paused for a moment, then continued. 'Lee went quiet, just glared at John.'

'What did he mean?'

'Nobody seems to know what John meant, except maybe John and Marge. Probably it meant nothing. Who knows? John's a vindictive man. Maybe it was the best way to shatter Lee on the night, even if it was a lie. My mother thinks that Lee doesn't know what he meant, and Lee never tried to find out.'

'Did Lee finish school?'

'No. He went mad. Something in his nature. The brightest boy in class did badly at school, got into more trouble with the law over drugs and, when police arrested him for the second time, his father refused to visit him in the remand centre. Lee got out. John hounded him to work harder at school. Lee worked less. When John and Marge demanded that he come home early, he came home late. Finally, he quit school and did labouring jobs around Bathurst, then announced to everyone in town, so the news would reach his parents second-hand, that he'd accepted a plumbing apprenticeship. Plumbers had accepted him as one of their own, even if Mum and Dad hadn't. John was shocked and hurt.'

'Secession,' said Julia.

'A few years ago, Lee got tired of Bathurst, and came to live in our white shining city.'

'With us.'

'Yes,' said Kate, 'with us.'

'How do you know all this?'

'I told you, from my mother.'

'She seems to remember a lot.'

'Some of it jogged her memory.'

Julia heard a door open. 'I have to go.'

'I'll ring you at work tomorrow.'

'Tomorrow's fine, but the day after we're on strike.'

'Strike? You have it easy.'

'Ruth's going to the strike meeting. Jeremy and I are driving to Mount Franklin with a friend of his, to check out an old ski lodge for the school camp.'

'Take Rose along.'

'No, not this time. I don't know her well enough.'

'Take her anyway.'

'No.'

'Anyway, I'll see you on Thursday. Please be there, don't forget.'

'How could I forget?'

'Sleep well,' she said.

Julia hung up the phone, and the way Kate said 'Sleep well' meant she wouldn't sleep well at all.

'Was that your work, Mummy?'

'Yes, well, sort of darling. It's my friend from the university talking about a girl in my class. The only girl I have, besides you.'

'Why's there only one girl?'

'Oh, its a special class. I'll take you to meet her one day.'

Claire read in a high clear voice, but she noticed that her mother wasn't listening. Kate's voice hung in the room, warm and dark. It pacified Julia and made her distant. Claire looked up and Brian stood just inside the kitchen door, hands deep in his pockets.

11

Eagle

After a week, Lee Cavanaugh walked into Jeremy's office. Rose stood behind him, obscured by his shadow. Lee came in the same brown striped shirt with his belly poking through the bottom buttons, and the same discoloured jeans he'd worn a week ago before. Waves of nicotine came off him; his fingertips were stained yellow. Rose wore a mantle of anger, eyes spitting hatred, mouth turned down. In a beige T-shirt and jeans with holes stitched up, she stared past Julia, and Julia's betrayal.

'Good morning.' Julia tried to offer some warmth.

'Morning. How are we today?' said Lee.

Jeremy said, 'Mrs Cavanaugh couldn't come this morning?'

'Uh, no. Got a headache.'

Jeremy leaned close to him. 'Nothing serious, I hope.'

'No, no. She's fine.'

Julia looked at Rose. 'You okay today?'

Rose tipped her face and mumbled something into the floor.

Jeremy said to Rose, 'Can we go through the rules again?'

She frowned.

For ten minutes of talk, Rose sat without moving. She'd left them long ago, signalling a switch-off, and Lee's attention had waned, his eyes glazing over as he looked through Julia and around the room.

'Rose,' said Julia, 'Jeremy has something he wants to show you.'

Jeremy reached behind his chair and pulled out a large cardboard box with a white towel over the top. He slowly peeled back the towel, gradually pouring light into the corners of the box and a downy white mound inside that rhythmically breathed up and down.

'What is it?' asked Lee. 'It's twice the size of a full-grown chook.'

'It's a wedge-tailed eagle chick. She's weak now, starving. Her parents were poisoned near Gundaroo. She was blown off the nest, apparently trying to find scraps of food on the edge.'

'Isn't she pretty?' Lee's eyes locked on the box.

The eagle with coal black pupils sat absolutely still, except for the breathing, hunkered down with four humans looming over it.

Jeremy said, 'The problem is she's broken her wing, Rose, the humerus, this large bone that goes into the body here.'

Jeremy touched Rose's upper arm. She didn't pull away.

Then he reached down and touched a finger of his right hand deep into the eagle's white down. 'The vet put a metal pin through here, through the two broken pieces of humerus, and he said we can take it out in three weeks. Birds heal quickly. But we'll keep her here and hand-feed her to bring up her weight. Otherwise she'll die.'

Lee peered into the box and listened, 'You have to train her to hunt then, don't you? Saw a film about that. Put leather on her legs, blind her eyes with a hat and fly her to your glove.'

'No, Lee. That film's nonsense. After she's healed and strong enough, we'll find a nest for her in the wild. If the parent eagles have young, they'll accept her and raise her as their own. She's not a pet really. When her wing's healed, she has to go.' Jeremy looked at Rose, 'I was hoping you could help me feed and care for her.'

Her eyes widened and she forgot momentarily to sulk. But she caught herself and retained enough hate to ignore Jeremy's offer, tried to maintain a sleepy look of disdain. She stared into the face of the snowy white eaglet lying in the box on the floor, her eyes as blank as a cat's.

Jeremy watched Rose and seemed confused about whether his offer had registered. He leaned forward to catch her eyes, and said in his syrupy drawl, 'The eagle can stay at my place at night, I'll bring her in each day.'

Rose struggled with her sulk. Eyes widening again from a sleepy squint as she stared into the box. Her voice whispering low and flat, 'Maybe.'

Lee stretched down and touched the eaglet 'Isn't it lovely? This'll be good fun, Rose.' The eagle lay still. 'But I don't think it's such a good idea putting her into another nest. Don't think the parents will feed her after she's been touched by humans.'

Jeremy looked irritated. He pushed his wire-rimmed glasses onto the bridge of his nose, shook his head a little and tossed off his 'I've-heard-this-one-a-thousand-times-before' look. 'That's not quite right, Lee. Parent eagles are happy to accept another nestling, and they don't mind if people handle their young. But they don't feed a nestling that's weak or sick, like this one. Rose and I will have to make her strong before we place her up in a new nest.'

Rose sat back in her chair and looked out the window. Julia worried about Lee's contaminating influence. Rose, she thought, would never touch anything that Lee had touched.

Jeremy pulled the box away into his lap, away from Lee's dirty hand. 'We shouldn't disturb her too much now,' he murmured softly. 'I'll settle her in the next room where it's quiet.' He looked at Rose. 'Why don't you come in next door, sit with her and keep her settled.'

He handed the box over to her. She spread her arms wide to receive it and Jeremy followed her next door.

Julia turned to Lee. 'How's Rose at home?'

'Fine, fine,' he said, and reached up and smoothed his hair across his skull. 'I sent her to her room when she came home from school last week, and she missed dinner. That'll make her think next time.' He nodded, reassuring Julia.

'I hope you didn't mind the other day,' said Julia. 'I had to mention her fears about going home, and Welfare. We need to be careful.'

His grey eyes shifted sideways. 'No, no. It's fine,' he said, and folded his arms over his chest. 'You just keep telling me what she's doing wrong, and I'll punish her. I guess a lot of kids here tell lies. You know how to tell when she's lying, don't you? She lies all the time. I don't hit her, nothin' like that, just send her to her room, make her think about what she's done wrong. The kid doesn't think…'

Julia drifted off, thinking about how Lee displayed these shining intentions through slippery talk, how nobody would believe anything he said because he was oily. His theme was that he, not Rose, was the victim of deceit, an honest man trapped in a dishonest world by a dishonest teenager. She was a liar.

'Lee…' she interrupted, 'we'd like to make a home visit sometime, if that's all right. Probably I'd come with Dr Kate Selby from the university. What day's convenient?' Julia leaned closer, trying to pierce his face and reveal what lay behind it, catch him off-guard with all his bullshit and self-serving fibs and put him on the back foot. 'In fact, Lee, we'd like to meet you and Holly every two weeks.'

His eyes flickered to the left, not too much. He was obviously practised at lying. But his deceit leaked through like grease through newspaper wrapped around deep-fried chips. He stared back, trying to fake it. 'Uh, well, okay. I guess, but, you know, we ah, we like to keep things to ourself. You know, you've got your work here at the school, we've got our family business at home. Family's family.'

'That's true, Lee, but we like to do the same things at school that you do at home, so Rose doesn't get confused.'

When Jeremy walked in from next door, Lee slumped in the low-backed chair as if outnumbered.

'Well, uh, look. If it's going to help Rose, then we'll just have to see.'

'Fine. We'll be in touch then. Thanks for coming in this morning.'

Julia stood up, held his gaze, smiled and shook his hand as firmly as she could. 'Oh, and Lee. We're on strike tomorrow, so Rose will have to stay home.'

'Yeah, fine.'

She motioned Lee towards the door and followed him. She walked beside him down the hall past the classroom.

He looked in at Rose leaning over the cardboard box murmuring quietly. Lee rested his hand on the doorway and called out, 'See you then, kid.'

Rose didn't look up.

12

Pigs

Park Ranger Mel Davidson had a gang-gang emblem sewn on his sleeve. He steered the Toyota through narrow-leafed peppermints and their milk chocolate bark, up through mountain gums, ribbon gums, and brown barrel on the road to Mount Franklin. Jeremy sat in the front seat with his friend, and Julia sat in the back. They straddled a rocky spine, the border between the Australian Capital Territory on the left and New South Wales on the right. A dozen yellow-tailed black cockatoos slow-flapped over the steep forest, squawking like rusty iron gates. Three jade and blood-coloured king parrots flashed over the road into a huddle of snow gums.

'How d'ya get out of the meeting?' asked Mel.

Jeremy said, 'Every other teacher in Canberra's there. Nobody will miss us.'

They bounced through potholes filled with standing water and pulled up to an old two-storey wooden ski lodge surrounded by sparse woodland and alpine heath in high clean air.

There was a slight breeze stirring in the eucalypts, rattling their hard leaves like rosaries. Julia reached into the back of the Toyota for her jacket, put it on and zipped it. A sugary scent wafted up from the earth. They walked over and looked through dirty windows in the lodge, shielding their eyes and peering at yellow dust and cobwebs inside.

'You can bring sleeping bags and food here for the kids, and something to cook,' said Mel, 'and you'll be set. There's beds and a stove in there, quite comfy. Spent a couple of nights up here myself.'

They circled the building.

Mel showed them the outhouse and the woodpile. 'There's two rooms for the kids upstairs, and you'll need a fire at night. It's cold. Want to look inside?'

He unlocked the door and they followed him in. It was cooler out of the sun, and it smelled like damp wood and mouldy paper.

Julia looked into the smaller bedroom. 'Rose, Ruth, and I can sleep in here, Jeremy. You and the boys can have the two large rooms.'

They stepped back outside and Jeremy said, 'Let's walk up the hill.'

They started up the rough, stony path to the top of Mount Franklin, trudging between snow gums twisted out of thin rocky ground. Near the top they came into a low, dark heath.

Suddenly Mel crouched, pumping his left hand down with his open palm. 'Pigs,' he whispered, 'keep down, don't move.'

He pointed to a clearing in open heath down the opposite hillside, and four tiny black forms. They trotted forward with their snouts on the ground, snuffled and flung up black clumps of sod. They must have been five hundred metres away.

'We're downwind, they won't smell us,' said Mel. 'I'll get the .308 from the truck, and circle round to get upwind. Stay where I can see you.'

Julia looked at Jeremy, her voice low. 'I don't want to see this.'

'He has to shoot them,' Jeremy whispered, 'part of his job.'

'Fine. I'll go back to the truck and read a book.' Julia started to stand up.

'No. It's best if you stay. We could ruin his chances if the pigs see us.' Jeremy handed the binoculars over and said, 'Have a look.'

Julia took them, squatting, and she could see the four pigs move in jerky steps, a loose gaggle over open ground.

'How does a vegetarian know so much about killing?' said Julia.

'If you grow up in America, you learn to kill animals just after you learn to walk. I was a National Rifle Association member before I turned nine. They attach ceremonies to your first kills, rites of passage. Read Faulkner.'

'No. That's part of the reason I don't.'

They looked down at Mel, far ahead now, stooped and loping fast over the hillside between clusters of squat snow gums. Through binoculars, Julia saw Mal crouch low, bobbing over the heath towards the pigs with the rifle slung close to the ground. The pigs kept shovelling with their snouts down leaving black soil upturned behind them. A wind blew Julia slightly off balance as Mel closed on the pigs.

'I can't understand why he's coming to them upwind.' Jeremy seemed to be talking to himself. 'Why don't they smell him?' He crouched and watched.

'I don't understand why you want to watch a pig hunt.'

'I don't eat them,' he said. 'I watch them.'

It was uncomfortable squatting on the rocky hillside so Julia stood up slowly and leaned against a snow gum next to the path. She could see Mel creep up to the front pig in the group. Apparently he could see the pigs, but the stupid things couldn't see him. Either that, or they were Babes that had escaped from somebody's hobby farm down in the valley.

Suddenly, the lead pig threw up her snout, flung dirt and tangled roots into the snow grass; it snorted loud enough for them to hear five hundred metres away. Mel raised the rifle to his eye, pigs shoulder to shoulder bumping and bursting through heather, tails high, bumping into each other like nimble little black dodgem cars. The pigs were squealing to get away. Through binoculars, Julia saw a puff of dust come off the back of one pig's shoulder; it dropped and rolled. Mel pulled back the bolt on the rifle, up to his eye again as the crack of the first rifle shot arrived. Another pig ran towards Mel; it tumbled as he pulled back the bolt and jammed a cartridge into the breech. The crack of the rifle again, a second after the pig fell. He twisted, swung the barrel towards a third pig that scooted over the ground trying to reach cover on Mel's left. The retort came after he swung the rifle hard behind him, twisting his body towards the pig that was disappearing into heavy brush. Julia and Jeremy couldn't see what happened next, but Mel turned around and relaxed as they heard the rifle crack.

Julia's pulse started to slow as she lowered the binoculars. She'd stood next to Jeremy watching Mel kill four pigs.

Mel ambled uphill, closer now. They stood quietly, waiting for him.

As he came over the rise, Jeremy said, 'One got away.'

'Nobody got away. Four for four. Two got round the side, but I got them.'

'How did you choose which one to shoot first?' asked Jeremy.

'You shoot the big leader first, in this case a sow. That confuses the others. Then you shoot whoever you can. Surprised me there was a sow leading this bunch.'

Julia felt nauseous.

But Jeremy seemed obsessed. 'I don't understand why you approached them from upwind instead of downwind. 'Why didn't you hide your scent?'

Mel looked at him, smiled a little and said, 'There's rules about taking a mob of pigs, but each set-up is different. You've got to get between the pigs and cover.'

'Even upwind?' Jeremy seemed to wrestle with the downwind question, as if it was a principle of physics.

'It's better downwind at first. But then, as you get closer, you move between the pigs and cover. That turned out to be upwind with this mob. As soon as they smell you, they panic and run to the nearest cover. I was standin' in the nearest cover. They can't see you very well, eyes are pretty bad, so I use their bad eyesight. They ran right towards me to get to thick heath. I had to keep track of you, so I didn't shoot a member of the public, 'specially a psychologist. And I had to keep track of each pig, so none got away.'

'Does the poisoning work?,' asked Jeremy.

'Oh, shit yes,' Mel crunched his face up, like it was a dumb question. 'It used to be terrible up here, with dug-up ground and pig wallows everywhere, knee-deep in pig shit, but we're getting them down now. Anyway, I pulled them out in the open. We'll leave them to the wedgies. I'm going to eat that ham sandwich in the glovebox. I'm starved.'

Mel turned and started back down the path.

As they followed, Julia began to distrust the level of macho in him; he enjoyed this. 'Glad we don't have Rose Cavanaugh with us today,' she said.

Mel suddenly changed from the cool teller of tales; his eyes narrowed. 'No relation to Lee Cavanaugh, is she?'

'Yes,' said Jeremy, 'though relation isn't a word she'd use. How do you know him?'

'Small town. Don't have an affair in this town, you two. I'd know in a week.'

Julia looked at the mountaintops around them. 'This town?'

'You know him because he's having an affair?' said Jeremy.

Mel chuckled. 'No, though I s'pose he might be. I know him because he's a pig killer.'

'Pig killer?' said Jeremy. 'Here in Namadgi?'

Mel smiled again. 'Sometimes he hunts Namadgi. Mostly he hunts Kosciuszko. We try to catch him, and a few other shooters, but they turned it into sort of a game. Well, a game for them, and work for us. Five or six parties hunt with dogs. Use a border collie to listen and smell for pigs from the back of a truck. They turn the collie loose to find the mob, run it down, then turn loose two or three Rottweilers or bull terriers to catch the pigs and hold them.'

'How?' said Jeremy.

'What do you mean how? How do they hold it?'

'By the legs, what?'

'The bigger dogs hold the pig down by its ears.'

Julia started to feel sick again.

'What then?' said Jeremy.

'Kill it usually, but this Cavanaugh fellow has a new trick. He comes out with a coupla eighteen- or nineteen-year-old boys he can boss around. Somehow he's got keys to our gates, and the gates into Kosciuszko. Maybe a mate in the electricity authority. The electricity boys have to come through Namadgi and into Kosciuszko because of the dams and the city water supplies, so we leave a lock on the gate they can open. We change the locks, and Lee gets more keys. When the Kosciuszko boys put on reinforced locks and gates, Lee cuts them off with acetylene torches, or rams through gates in his Toyota. He's not the only one who does that.'

'What's Lee's special trick?' said Jeremy.

Mel glanced at Julia; he seemed to be thinking, 'How should a no-nonsense tough guy like me spell out the gory part in front of the girl?'

Jeremy said, 'What's the problem?'

He cleared his throat. 'These guys believe it's a sport, you see, their sport. Parks Service is trying to get rid of pigs, after all, so we're hypocrites. We try to get rid of pigs, but stop Lee and his friends shooting pigs. Rangers want all the fun for themselves, you see. These guys tell me that. I caught a group of them up here once, by myself. They surrounded me, pushed me up against a tree. Wasn't Lee's mob, it was another bunch. They knew I couldn't do anything in court without witnesses.'

'And Lee?'

'He sees it as civil disobedience. He's determined to keep pigs running in my park, and in Kosciuszko.'

'Tell us about Lee's trick,' said Jeremy.

'They hold drunken weekends up here, stand around the fire with stubbies in their hands and talk about women and pig killing, in the same breath. And their hatred of us. When his dogs catch a pig, he and his mates hold it down, squealing and kicking. They have this little ceremony. Not sure whether they name the pig after one of us, or one of their women, but they cut its ears off.'

'What?' Julia said.

'Then they hold down the squealing pig and carve someone's name into its hide with a hot knife. I found my name on one, and the name Betty on one, the wife of a young guy who comes out with Lee. They finish the ceremony, hold the dogs, and turn the pig loose.'

'How do you know all this?' said Jeremy.

'I've caught them at it, but, like I said, with no back-up I can't take them to court. They piss off before I can get the cops up here.'

For a moment, nobody spoke.

'Let me explain something. You see, the pig's really wary of humans after that, harder to catch or shoot. More important, when a rival pig-hunting group sets their dogs after that pig, the dogs grab for the pig's ears, and there's no ears to grab.'

'So what happens?' said Julia.

'The dogs get sliced up, sometimes badly. Lee and his mates think it's funny. Pigs are nasty when they're cornered. That's one reason I wanted you to stay back today. If the dogs can't hold onto the ears, there's not much else to hold on to on a pig. Pigs are sort of round, you see. The pig turns on the dogs with its tusks and cuts them. Lee's rivals had some dogs cut up, one died, and it was Lee's little joke. I know these earless pigs keep breeding, because I shoot them. That sow I just shot's got "Norma" carved on it. That's not Lee's wife, is it?'

'Watch for "Holly",' said Jeremy, or "Rose".'

They went quiet. Mel walked between them until they arrived at the four-wheel drive parked in snow gums. He opened the truck to let them in. Julia climbed into the back seat and Mel flipped open the glovebox for his ham sandwich. He ate as he started the Toyota and drove down off Mount Franklin. They coasted with gravel snapping under the Toyota's hard tires, the gearbox whining. They truck pitched around corners and nobody spoke.

Julia sat in the back seat thinking about pigs.

13

Jeremy

Rose leaned over the clean white nestling, murmuring, urging her to lift her head and open her black beak for food. The eagle lay with its eyes closed for most of the day. During that week, Rose spent more time on the grass outside Julia's window encouraging the eagle to sit up and stretch its big yellow-white feet in front of her. But it refused to eat and Jeremy spoke in low undertones to Julia about failure. When Julia pressed him, he stood quietly in the bone-coloured classroom, glassy-eyed and seemingly afraid of her questions. Though he tried to explain it as a hiccup, a minor setback, his speech was stumbling and uncertain. He talked this way for most of that week and by Friday he said the nestling would probably die. Their plans to help Rose with a companion, a story about healing and growth and freedom, a ceremony of deliverance, had faltered and turned bad.

The following day, the eagle was no better and Jeremy had changed his mind about words to use with Rose. He would tell her that death was part of the cycle, and understanding this would leave her strong and help her move forward. She would know that she had cared with pure intentions and failed, that nothing more could be done, and she would remember this time with pride. Failure in nature wasn't so much a failure as natural law, part of Darwin's plan. It doesn't hollow out the pit of your stomach like social failure does.

Julia thought about his defence of failure and tried to believe him but couldn't. He had tried to put a positive light on Rose's heartbreak and failed to convince anyone. As she slept, Julia had a recurring dream over that fortnight, almost every night, a simple, obvious dream where

Rose floated in a small boat with Jeremy and Julia, then suddenly tipped herself into the water and drifted and spun, like a silver spoon, disappearing to the jade-coloured bottom. Jeremy and Julia reached out to catch her but only caught a handful of snow.

Each day, Rose isolated herself in the corner of the yard and worked at persuading the eagle to eat. With extended hands, she pleaded. She never wept, even as the eagle weakened and the end was clear.

Jeremy would shut his office door and plan with Julia how to manage the steps of bereavement that Rose would certainly move through.

Though she was sick, the eagle's feathers continued to grow. Her face had small brown feathers on the cheeks. Large quill feathers poked out of her tail and the trailing edges of her wings making her half brown, half white. She lay there sick, and grew feathers. Tiny parachutes of shed white down lay scattered over the schoolyard like sugary blossoms. They floated into bushes and fastened there, plumes that would stay for weeks after the eagle was buried, a reminder of lost hope. When the boys came too close to the basket, the eagle rocked back onto her short tail and freed her feet so she could skirmish with them and lash out with her black talons and cut them.

She always welcomed Rose with a high, sweet piping and Jeremy had taught Rose to follow certain conventions that gained the eagle's trust. 'Creep in low from an angle,' he said, 'oblique, low and slow, crouching with respect. Look to the side, never directly at her. Watch the eagle out the corner of your eye. Like this.'

Rose mimicked him.

'As you near the basket, sit on the ground, low and safe for her. Talk to her. Say, "It's me. Don't be afraid."'

The following day, Jeremy walked slowly to the basket and sat on the ground next to Rose. 'How do you think she looks?'

Without looking up, Rose said, 'She doesn't eat.'

'Keep trying. She trusts you, and she'll take more food as she feels better.'

'How long before then?'

'I don't know. If she makes it, we'll put her up in the nest in three weeks. You can come along.'

'Can I?'

'You have to understand that she may not live. But, if she does, the ranger Mel Davidson found a nest, and he said he'd climb it for us.'

'What if she doesn't live?'

'Well, let's worry about that if it happens. But we don't know at the moment if she'll live or not.'

Jeremy touched the eagle's beak. 'You're still trying to feed her at 10, 1 and 3, aren't you?'

'She doesn't eat.'

'Just keep trying at those times.'

From the saucer lying on the grass, she lifted a small raw strip of rabbit in her fingers. She held it close to the eagle's black beak, flopped the meat near its sharp tip. The eagle lay still.

With Jeremy sitting by her side, Rose pleaded in a soft voice, 'Please. Just one piece. It's good.' She looked up at Jeremy, 'She won't take it.'

'Just be gentle, like you naturally are, make it safe for her. Keep trying. When she trusts you, she'll eat.'

'She trusted me last week.'

'She trusts you now, but she's sick.'

'Sometimes I want her to come home with me, but mostly I don't.'

'The licence says she has to stay with me until she's released.'

'Come on,' she said to the eagle. 'Just one piece. I'm your friend.'

The eagle lay quietly with its black eyes open.

'Please,' said Rose, and the eagle reached up slowly, wobbling, it faltered, then reached up again, pulled slowly at a sliver of pink rabbit in Rose's fingers.

The eagle flipped her head back once, twice, three times, then swallowed.

'Good girl. Now another one,' said Rose, and she pulled off a sliver and held it to the eagle's beak. The eagle watched Rose, then slowly opened its beak again, with Rose pursing her lips and cooing to her, 'You're a good girl.'

'You have a natural gift,' said Jeremy.

She looked up at him, surprised at what he'd said, then back down to the saucer for another sliver of meat.

'I need to go inside,' said Jeremy, 'to see Julia. Call me if you need help.'

Rose watched him stroll across the yard into the school.

Looking out the window, he said to Julia, 'She's very good. Animals trust her.'

'I'd like to know what she's thinking.'

'Probably not much. She's driven to care for someone else's offspring. Surely you get that.'

'Barely. The immediate problem for us is to plan what happens if the eagle dies. And what's Bob going to say, and what's Bob going to do when he finds out we had an eagle at school, and it died?'

'No idea.'

'He'll face mutiny if he tries to stop us. Most of the time, he doesn't know what goes on here. We do what we like, until he finds out about it.'

'You know the line. He's ultimately responsible. He needs to know the sources of complaint from the public about his school, before the complaint reaches him, or the newspapers.'

As they stood talking, Rose leaned over the basket, murmuring softly, too softly for them to hear. She wasn't feeding it any more; the eagle rested low in the basket with her eyes closed. Rose sat by the nestling and told her secrets that she wouldn't tell Julia, touched her feathered back and gestured with her left hand as she whispered.

'I have to go,' said Jeremy. 'You're all right with Rose, aren't you?'

'Yes. You prepared for tonight?'

'Sort of.'

'See you there.'

Jeremy turned and walked out the door.

When Julia gave Rose the book of stories and coloured drawings that Marlene had given her ten years before, she pored over them all day, held the book on her desk so fixed on what Marlene had written and thought and believed that Julia had to remind her to feed the eagle at 3.

Julia didn't know how to talk to Rose, felt as if coils of barbed wire lay between them, a fence of broken glass. What Rose made of Marlene's book Julia didn't know, and she sometimes wondered if she, Julia, assumed that Rose was deeper and more complicated in her silences than she really was. Teachers in the unit assumed depth and contemplation in all of the children, that girls like Rose had known a continuity of suffering and ugly humiliation that other children hadn't known, so they had insight that other children could never match. With these children the teachers sweated blood over, lost weight over, sacrificed their looks and sleep over, they had to believe there was insight and wisdom and hope in their stillness. In their blank stares these children must be contemplating good and evil.

In the afternoon, Rose came back inside and watched as Julia sent the boys off. 'Peter, when you become chief minister, don't forget to tell them how nicely we treated you here.'

He didn't look round.

Rose walked to her desk, picked up Marlene's book, then came and stood next to her. 'Can I take it home?'

'I'd rather you didn't. I know you understand. If you ever wrote something for me, I couldn't lend it out.'

'Do you know,' she asked, 'what the raven told Marlene when she went to see her uncle?'

'It was a secret. My understanding was that the raven explained to her uncle why Marlene went crazy, about the bone missing her mother and stabbing Marlene in the breast, and the raven told the uncle what should be done about it.'

'Do eagles do that?'

To Julia it was a strange question, but she tried to answer, 'In Marlene's story, people got power and wisdom from the raven, but I know that other families got power, wisdom, and advice, from the eagle; eagles offered counsel. Do you want me to get some books on it?'

One of the many habits, thought Julia, that make teachers so boring to children.

'If you want.' Rose turned from her desk, picked up her school bag, and walked to the bus stop.

That night, Julia saw Kate. Every month, the local ornithologists met down at the Griffin Centre, and Kate and Julia decided to go, as an excuse to be with each other. That night Jeremy was the main speaker. Julia needed an excuse to leave the house. She felt good that she told Brian she had gone to hear Jeremy speak, which she had.

They could hear warm chatter as they arrived. Two hundred, mainly elderly, members sat in arced rows of chairs. Kate and Julia would find a place up the back to hide.

None of the members knew Julia or Kate, and that was lucky because they planned to sneak away early in the night. Kate brought a novel, *Notes from Underground*.

'If we're leaving early,' said Julia, 'you don't need that.'

'Just in case.'

Jeremy met them at the door, and he seemed to know why they'd come. They trusted him to protect their secret. Kate and Julia sat close to each other.

Jeremy's lover, a maths teacher named Alan Morrison, came in and sat in the back row near them. Julia nodded as he passed. One afternoon last year when Alan had picked up Jeremy after school, he laid his hand on Jeremy's shoulder as they got into the car. Julia felt the muscles in her sternum tighten and she furtively glanced around to see if the boys had seen what she had seen. Later she felt bad that she had been so uneasy about a sign of natural affection, but parents in the

1990s would have driven Jeremy out of Wattle Street if they'd known, and it would have made the newspapers.

On the fringe of the night's ornithologists' meeting, back where nobody could see them, Kate leaned over to Julia. 'How many of these people have made love outside in broad daylight?'

'Probably more than you'd guess.'

The lights went out for members to show slides, and Kate kissed the side of Julia's mouth. Julia could recognise the fine, sweet musk of her body in a darkened room full of people. Two latecomers arrived. The opening door threw a wedge of light into the room and Julia couldn't see them clearly, and hoped they didn't know her.

A woman stood up and related, in some detail, her adventure with a rare honeyeater.

Kate leaned over to Julia and said, 'Don't make any sudden movements. She's probably more frightened of us than we are of her of her.'

Julia raised her finger to her lips.

The middle-aged thick-set woman with grey hair cut like a schoolboy's, dressed in shorts and walking boots, stood for five minutes and told the meeting about the rare Lewin's honeyeater she'd spotted, where it was, and how the others could find it. She'd be the sort of woman who'd keep her guests captive in her sitting room for hours on a Sunday afternoon with photos of her dog.

Kate smiled and squeezed Julia's hand. 'You know,' she whispered, 'the right to free speech doesn't give people the right to be taken seriously. She's far too earnest. She'd punch someone who said her identification was mistaken.'

'Like fights in your department.'

'Not quite. Fights in my department are different. They're about nothing. We're paid good tax dollars to fight about nothing. These people fight for free.'

'Good point. Jeremy talks for free.'

Kate laid her hand on Julia's thigh. 'It makes me uncomfortable when Jeremy's so new-age, and noble, and full of charity. How long do we have to sit here and watch it on display?'

'Not long, darling. Just ride it out.'

Kate leaned back and tried to read her novel in the light reflected off Jeremy's slides.

14

Casework

The fight came in Thursday's meeting, a meeting that served to remind teachers at Wattle Street that Bob considered their casework decisions laughable. And he wanted to be let in on the joke.

The day was breathless, as calm as a prayer. The sky was a glossy blue. Inside they were restless on children's low-backed chairs with morning light falling on papers and files on their laps. Jeremy came in flapping with folders, patting his breast pocket looking for his glasses. He stood in the doorway organising himself. Kate sauntered in troubled and frowning, a half a head taller than Jeremy. She opened two paper bags, set out on the table croissants, orange juice and jam to eat during the meeting. Ruth didn't look up.

Julia was disturbed when Kate walked in, thrown into confusion by the look she gave, by an angry phrase she imagined on Kate's lips. Kate was tense and bothered about something, as if in a shadow; her silence carried an edge and Julia wondered if she'd woken in the deep of night and been too irritable and displaced to fall asleep again. Julia had failed yesterday to meet her on Black Mountain. Julia wanted to cradle her face, keep her warm and feed her, but she hid her impulse well and nodded impersonally to her lover.

'Who's on the agenda today?' said Bob, reaching for a croissant.

Julia said, 'Rose.'

'Okay, let's go.' Bob seemed to fill the room with his body as he wiped crumbs from the side of his mouth.

'Her first two weeks weren't bad,' said Julia, 'though we had to send her home on the first day. Excuse me if I'm less than professional, but her stepfather's pretty greasy and scary.'

'Doesn't scare me,' said Ruth.

'When Lee came to get Rose, she recoiled, she didn't want to be touched by him, or even be in the same room with him.'

Bob was slow to appreciate what Julia was saying, and the others were distracted by crumbs stuck to a spot of toothpaste on his mouth. He looked at Jeremy. 'Got any more on that?'

'Not much, I'm afraid.' Jeremy had located the lost glasses; they were on his face, and he could see his notes more clearly now. 'Welfare's on the case. They think she was interfered with, or is currently being interfered with by someone, and they'll give us new information when they get it. They want help from us, including reports of anything Rose says that's relevant to their ongoing investigation.'

Bob frowned. 'Why don't the police just take him in?'

Jeremy shook his head. 'Rose and her mother deny it. So the police can't question Lee, or charge him.'

Julia could see Ruth tighten the pencil in her fist, and repeatedly stab the page on the desk in front of her.

'What do we do?' said Bob. 'Wait around? Want me to have a talk to this guy? What's his name again?' He looked at each of them in turn.

'Lee,' said Jeremy. 'No, I think we gather more information first, and wait for the police. Julia?'

'I agree.'

'Julia sent him a little message the other day,' said Jeremy.

Bob knitted his brow. 'A message?'

'Told him that Rose started wailing, that she was frightened of being sent home because he would beat her, and that Welfare wanted to know if he did beat her.'

'Ah yes,' said Bob, 'I know that one, the old good cop, bad cop trick. Not sure that's such a good idea in this case. He'll threaten to beat the kid harder – "Keep quiet kid, or else."'

Kate pulled a strand of hair aside with a fingernail and leaned forward. 'I suspect that he threatens her anyway, Bob. Julia tried to form an alliance with Lee, distasteful as that may sound, and, at the same time, protect Rose. It's not the good cop, bad cop trick.' Kate was able to make these events sound planned and elegant, not soft-minded and contrived on the spot as they usually were.

Bob sat unconvinced. 'Well, what happened? Did Rose get a hidin'?'

'She won't talk about home,' said Julia, 'and that's one of the problems. But no, I'm pretty sure she didn't get beaten when she got home.'

'Okay,' said Bob, 'what else?' He looked around at the room and back at Julia.

'I asked Lee about a home visit,' said Julia, 'and I told him Kate would come along. Sorry, Kate, I forgot to tell you. Is that all right?'

Kate sat gazing at Julia, her face intense. Ruth looked at Kate, then back at Julia. The stillness continued, nobody spoke. Julia hoped that too many seconds hadn't passed. She realised that Kate wasn't going to answer.

'Anyway,' said Julia, 'Lee got evasive when I mentioned a home visit. He finally agreed, maybe to escape talking to me any longer. He wanted to get out the door. And oh, Jeremy, can you say something about the baby eagle?'

'Eagle!' Bob nearly stood up. 'What does Jeremy have to do with an eagle?'

'The eagle was my idea,' said Kate, taking the heat out of Jeremy's surprise. 'But let's start with the home visit. Kate leaned back in and said, 'Julia, I can go to the Cavanaughs with you. Let's do it soon, this week if possible, because Lee doesn't want it to happen. So we make it happen, pressure him. We can't deliver long-term success with children like Rose unless we do something about the family. Maybe Rose should be out of that home.'

'Fine,' said Bob, 'take her out of the home. Whatever. Now what about this eagle?'

Kate smiled. 'Well, as you know, Jeremy has other expertise besides counselling. We thought it could help if he brought in a raptor rehab case. Rose could raise and release an orphaned animal. Something to make school attractive for her, and something to help us communicate with her.'

Jeremy cleared his throat. 'It's…ah…I was told about this young eagle blown from its nest after the parents were poisoned, killed. It has a broken wing so it will take some time to heal. It needs to be fed for three weeks or so, and Rose can help us, then go with us when we place the eagle in a nest on the river.'

Ruth sat in reserve, folding her arms and ready to spring at Bob like a Doberman if he said no.

Julia said, 'The eagle stays at Jeremy's house and comes in during the school day. Rose doesn't trust me, because I sent her home on the first day. She's talking to Jeremy, and –'

'I don't like it,' said Bob as he held up his second croissant and pointed the unbitten end at Julia. Speaking with his mouth half full, 'Check the regulations, you know,' he chewed, and had trouble with the words animal lib and Health Department. 'Eagles are dangerous.'

'They are.' Jeremy's quiet Yankee voice showed an edge. 'They can hurt you with their talons even at this age. But I'm watching, and she's smart about animals. She doesn't threaten the eagle, so it doesn't defend itself against her. Besides, the eagle's quite sick, it may not live.'

'What? Oh, great,' said Bob, 'just great. Even better. The kid dodges its talons for a couple of weeks, then goes into Calvary with avian pox. What are we running here?'

Ruth leaned forward, the dotting on the pad in front of her had now formed a crimson rosette. She pointed the end of her pen at him. 'Look, Bob.'

He swivelled in his seat and faced her.

'I've seen this kid with the eagle and it's wonderful, just wonderful. She pats it, talks to it, comes to my room about it, feeds it. The sort of thing we just don't see in this place. Never. It's stopped the boys fighting so much. If you don't support this project, Bob, I'll be very angry, very disappointed in you. Expect trouble from all of us, Bob.'

He sat back, confused for a moment, stopped chewing, and said, 'Then tell me, Ruth. As principal, and the man in charge of this... this zoo. What happens if it gouges someone's eye out? Why didn't someone tell me?'

The answer lay on Ruth's lips. 'Because you're never here.' She understood his backward-sloping indifference to work. She understood his strong dislike for children, his contempt for coal-face teachers. But not complaints from the public. She knew Bob was about to say 'No.'

'Look,' said Julia, 'I'm sorry, this was my fault. I spoke to Kate about it, then Jeremy and I thought you'd support it, then I lost track of the time. It's my fault. I should have phoned you.'

Bob was seldom clear about what to say or do when he knew full well he was being conned. He couldn't think quickly enough in meetings. He frowned, chewed on the end of his croissant.

Ruth stared at him. 'Bob?'

'This sort of thing can't happen again.'

'It won't,' said Julia.

'Okay, okay.' Red-faced and fractious, he sat back and fumed. 'I'll see what I can do. No, no, I'll think about it. I'll think about it. Let's keep moving. What's next?'

Jeremy shuffled through papers on his lap. 'I had a cup of tea with Peter Clark's mother this week.'

Julia thought about the apricot-haired mother of Peter Clark, the red-haired, snotty-nosed, bad-breathed boy with too many head colds and the big square teeth. He'd been there for six months.

'She phoned and seemed to want to talk. She broke down and said things were rocky in the marriage. Peter's father's lost his job, spends his time at home, and she's having an affair with a guy at work. She didn't know whether to tell her husband or not, didn't know if she would move out of the house and in with the new guy or not. Looks like they'll split up anyway.'

Kate leaned forward. 'Probably the cause of school troubles with most of the students here, it's just hidden for a while. The research shows that economic downturns, like the current sackings in the public service, cause a lot of marital discord, and this causes antisocial behaviour in schools.'

Everyone but Ruth turned and listened.

'My PhD supervisor once told me that the key to uncovering family discord is to interview the family's youngest member, alone. The youngest member is more likely to reveal secrets about splits, betrayal, and fighting inside the family than older members who deny any conflict and protect the family's integrity…'

'Come on, Kate,' said Ruth, 'we don't need this.' She looked at her watch. 'I mean, really. Surprise, surprise. Our kids come from broken homes. Kate tells us that our boys come from broken homes. Really? Don't waste our time. Some of us have to teach in ten minutes.'

Nobody dared to look at Kate as Ruth continued. 'Don't tell us what we already know. Tell us what we need to *do* about it. That's what you're here for. What do we *do*?' She shook her head. 'Really.'

Kate smiled, a forced smile Julia thought, 'Okay, Ruth.'

But Ruth pointed with a shaky index finger, 'After you people leave, we're alone in this place.'

'You look,' said Bob. He pointed a croissant at Ruth. 'I have to go back to the main school in two minutes. Someone, I don't know who but I plan to find out, pinned up a sign up in the staffroom – "All care but no responsibility taken with your children". A parent saw it, and there's gonna be trouble. I don't think that's funny. Do you think that's funny?'

'No,' said Julia, but she obviously did.

'Not funny at all,' said Jeremy.

Ruth hunkered down with her arms folded and Kate folded her hands in her lap. They didn't look at each other.

'Well, that's the sort of thing I mean. You bring an eagle into this school, now I've got to carry the can for those clowns across the way. Next I'll be carrying the can for you lot. What's next? Surprise me.' He stood up clutching his fourth croissant and hoisted his pants with the other hand, 'See ya next week.' He walked out.

Kate stood and stretched her fists towards the ceiling; she walked over to Julia. 'Can I see you for a minute?'

Julia looked at her, just a glance, 'Uh, for a minute.' She turned to Ruth. 'If I'm late, can you watch my kids?'

'Sure.'

They walked to her car, and looked back into the classroom. Nobody watched them. Julia could see Ruth's squat figure moving towards the door.

Kate leaned against her Volvo and gazed into Julia's face, the second time she'd done so that morning. 'What happened?' said Kate.

Julia backed away from Kate's edgy tone, her eyes and lips were tight. 'With Ruth, you mean?'

'No, no. To hell with that demonic Scot. Last night. I waited for half an hour in the Black Mountain car park.'

'Darling, you know what to do. Wait half an hour, then go. That's our agreement.'

'I don't care.'

'I'm sorry.'

'I sat there on a log on Caswell Drive and watched every car pass.'

'I'm sorry, darling.'

'A Mazda came over the crest of the hill, and by then, I didn't care if it contained you or Brian or the whole family. I was wild-eyed, standing there. Some young guy drove past.'

Julia waited.

'I was in despair,' said Kate. 'I decided to wait fifteen minutes, wondering if you were hurt, kidnapped, or you'd lost interest. I thought maybe I should trace the roads back to school and look for your Mazda, stalled, maybe crashed into a tree. How would I know?'

'I'm sorry.'

'I guess it was anger at being stood up. I didn't know what to do. You stood me up. It curdled my stomach, took on this life of its own. I don't know why, but I lost it. Another car rolled over the hill, I was hoping it was you. An old Toyota this time. I went berserk.'

'I'm sorry.'

'I sat down and cried. A few people saw me there.'

'I couldn't come. Ben was sick. He came home from school looking terrible, and Brian put him to bed. I couldn't come, I couldn't leave him. Surely you understand that.'

Kate studied her eyes, down her throat to her breasts. Some of the hurt drifted out of her face, but not all of it. 'I'm sorry,' she said. 'It's just that I had to see you. I needed to touch you, and when you didn't come, I thought, well, maybe something had happened. I thought maybe you were hurt, and I couldn't phone your house. There was no way I could find out what happened. I'm not sure how much longer I can do this.'

As they stood in the parking lot at the front of the school, a sharp wind circled and blew leaves around Julia's feet, plastered her dress into the crease of her legs. She listened and looked at Kate, and fought an urge to touch her face.

Kate looked down. 'I'm sorry. You're right. What can I say?'

'I knew you weren't well when you came in this morning.'

'Can we meet next week?'

'You know we can. I'll be there. And I love you, but I have to go now. I've been out here too long, my kids…'

'You'll phone me?' She looked beaten and vulnerable. Julia had never seen her so desolate.

'Of course I will. Are things bad at work?'

'Bad at work? They're pretty bad here. What are we going to do about that Scottish lunatic?'

'I don't know, she's –'

'All that hate sloshing around. It wears me down.'

'I'll ring you, then. We'll make a time.'

Kate looked as though a rock had lifted from her back; some of the shadow flowed out from the corners of her eyes. 'Bye,' she said. 'And, darling…'

'What?'

'Tell the demonic Scot that she didn't draw any blood this morning. Not a drop. She didn't even scratch me. Tell her to try harder next time.'

'She'll like that. It's like an analogy from Rob Roy.'

'And one more thing.'

'What?'

'Tell Bob those croissants were for everyone.'

Julia looked back at the school. 'He's a hungry boy and still growing. He'd take it better from you.'

She slid into her car, and Julia turned to walk back to her classroom, Ruth watching them from her window.

15

Forever

Julia emerged through high forest with the north wind at her back. She stepped around a spiky bush and slid between dappled trees and pulled a yellow flower down to her cheek. She crossed a rushing creek and watched the water scuttle over stones and tree roots. She climbed to the pine tree on the hill. Sun fired the western slope of the mountain, peeling eucalypt trunks looked like beaten copper. Wind lifted the hair from her shoulders and whipped it into the corners of her mouth.

Kate approached from below.

Julia sat with her knees tucked under her chin and watched. She stood and walked down the hill, slid her hand onto Kate's shoulder, and tucked her face into her neck. 'I missed you.'

'I missed you too.'

'In those meetings, I fight the desire to walk across the room and kiss your mouth.'

'Do it one day.'

'I've brought us a treat.'

They sat under the tree, and from her backpack Julia pulled a thermos of hot water, a small coffee plunger with ground coffee in the bottom, and two cinnamon rolls from the Viennese bakery in Civic. Julia poured hot water over the coffee, letting the steam rise into the cool air that Canberra gets in September during late afternoon. Julia set the glass plunger on rocky soil to brew against the tree. She held open the white bag of cinnamon rolls. 'Taste one.'

Kate pulled one out, bit into it, and handed it to Julia, who bit in after her, sticky sugar around the outside of her mouth.

Kate leaned over and licked icing from the corner of her lip. 'Having fun, aren't we?'

With her finger, Julia pushed icing into her mouth, 'I think so. How do you tell?'

'I'm not sure. How do you tell?'

Julia pulled two cups from the backpack, poured coffee and set the cups down steaming on the uneven forest floor. Red sun lay over Mount Painter and showed what time remained.

'This is wonderful,' she said, 'just wonderful.' She held up a cinnamon roll. 'Do you know, if we ran to Civic and back, we'd use up a tenth of the calories in one of these.'

'Who cares?'

'Not me.'

Julia packed the cups, coffee maker, and the bag with the last cinnamon roll into her backpack and pulled out a damp towel.

'Wait,' said Kate, 'wait,' and leaned over with shiny eyes and kissed Julia, licked the corner of her sugary mouth, and pulled a sprig of grass out of her hair. 'In primates, mutual grooming turns into gossip.'

'Ruth and I do that all day.'

'Well, Ruth's a special case. But we groom each other to keep track of who's on our side and who's not. Enemies, alliances. Track reputations. Who we can trust when the crunch comes. I'm lecturing again, aren't I?'

'You are. And I'd trust Ruth when the crunch comes. The families of kids in the unit live by harder rules than the rest of us, and Ruth understands that. She won't fold. Jeremy and the others might have pure intentions, but they have little backbone.'

'Yeah, well, now you're trying to redeem her for attacking me last week. I'm not sure where she evolved from. The selective pressures in Scotland are mysterious. It's strange how textbook Wattle Street is. Women evolved to band together and force men to invest in their own offspring. You do it for a living. The demonic Scot formed a hate bond with you to bring men to ground.'

'Problem is Lee doesn't see Rose as his own.'

'No, he doesn't.'

They finished, stood up and left.

Julia pranced up the hill and Kate followed. 'You have a lovely wiggle. Take your knickers off.'

Julia stood and looked over her shoulder, then lifted her long dress and slipped her white knickers down to her ankles and off. She reached over to her hip pocket and slid them in.

They turned and hiked further up the hill, Kate following Julia through a maze of scribbly gums.

'Lift your dress,' said Kate, and Julia walked and lifted it just enough to flash her bare bottom. Then she did it again.

The mountain poured red heat into their thighs as they coasted around the hill towards the crest and drank in the sharp smell of tea tree. They passed native cherries along the way, nibbled the red berries that rosellas had missed.

Holding hands, they ambled over the ridge toward the south side of the mountain.

'How are things at home?' asked Kate.

'Let's not ruin the afternoon.'

'Don't then.' She was irritated.

'Things are the same. Crushing grey boredom. We do our best to raise the kids and I long ago stopped making love to him because I stopped loving him.'

Kate walked beside her and seemed to listen, but said nothing.

'I like myself when I'm with you,' said Julia, 'and hate my body when I'm with him. The kids are innocent, and if you and I get hurt because of days like today, well, so be it. We deserve it. But the kids don't deserve it.'

Kate turned and watched the side of Julia's face.

Julia glanced back. 'Why do you stare at me like that?'

'Because you're beautiful.'

Julia shook her head. 'I don't think so.'

'And that's part of the reason you're so beautiful. You don't know it. Men turn and watch you in the street, and you don't even notice.'

'I don't care about men, or other women,' Julia said and turned and looked at bushland below them.

Kate said, 'The other day a young lad raised his hand, stood up and asked a question that made me realise he hadn't understood a word I'd said in the last hour. I couldn't answer his question because I'd have to start all over.'

'Only one person? Maybe the rest understood.'

'I don't know. They'd been looking at their watches, mumbling to each other. I lost them. Maybe I'm too sensitive, but I wonder if I lost them weeks ago and didn't notice. After the lecture, I went to the gym and pounded weights for an hour. But it didn't help, so I got drunk.'

'I'm sorry.'

Julia looked ahead as they pushed up hill. 'Let's go away and live together,' and as soon as it came out, she realised how stupid it was.

'I need to tell you something,' said Kate.

It was all too grave, and Julia didn't want sadness and melancholy in their time on the mountain. There was a sense of loss in Kate's voice.

'Go ahead.'

'You don't want to talk about this, do you?'

'If I say go ahead, I mean go ahead.'

They hiked in silence, anger pushing them.

Kate stopped and leaned against an apple box. 'I'll probably leave work, and it could be soon. They won't be surprised when I do it, but I needed to tell you.'

Julia felt a jolt in her chest, but looked ahead. She slipped her hand over Kate's shoulder.

Kate said, 'You'd like to put your kids out of the fighting, wouldn't you?'

'Like I said, it's not really a fight they're in, it's a morose grey room, a forlorn house. I'm sick of talking about my dead marriage. Let's talk about something else.'

'And I'm sick of talking about work.'

They ambled through forest without speaking, without being childish, or giddy lovers, or touching.

'Rose Cavanaugh?' said Julia. 'Can we talk about Rose, or maybe Lee?'

'Fine.'

'Are we going to their house next week? Can you get the time?'

'I'll make time. What night?'

'Tuesday?'

'Fine. We'll put some quiet pressure on Lee, so he thinks carefully about what he's doing to Rose.'

'You have a handsome face on the outside, but a menacing head on the inside.'

'Of course. I got a psychology degree so I could mess with people's heads.'

'That's why you're coming. Lee's a bully, and Jeremy doesn't scare him. You're coming along to scare him for me. Tuesday night then.'

'Done.'

'Two other things.'

'Ask away.'

'After we see the Cavanaughs, can we sneak into your house, maybe park at the end of the block?'

'Sure. What's the other thing?'

They looked at the lake below them, islands and tiny boats sailed by; figures sailing them looked like ants.

'How did bureaucrats ever create such a fine place?'

'Maybe they didn't. Maybe the whole town looks like shit to everyone else.'

'Maybe it does. But I don't think so.' Kate touched her face. 'Let me look at you.'

'Look at me under the tree.'

Mountain dusk settled around them as they drifted over the ridge, linked by warm hands, walking near the road. Sunset looked like a purple bruise.

'We'd better be careful,' said Julia, and dropped her hand.

Along the path, next to Julia with an arm over her shoulder, in the easy way that girls and boys did in the street, a breast pressing into her back. At a fork in the trail, Julia hesitated and turned left to go home; strong arms around her waist and warm breath in her ear as Kate whispered goodbye.

16

Thief

Two weeks later, Rose missed school again. Julia phoned her parents and Holly answered, paused for a moment and told her in the flat tones that broken people use.

'She went to school. Don't know where she got to after that.'

If Holly was concerned, it didn't show over the phone. Julia thanked her and told her they would follow it up.

After she was arrested, a security guard from Belconnen Mall, a sales girl named Jean from a clothing shop, and a police officer named Lisa Charles told Julia enough to piece together much of what happened that day, though Rose disputed parts of their stories.

She had wandered from the bus stop into the mall. Through the door, past the newsagent, the bookshop, browsing in Grace Brothers' window with the security guard now starting to watch her. Rose stared at thin cotton tops, belts, jeans and other clothes that she couldn't afford, and those watching her knew it.

'Bit underfed, isn't she?' said the security guard, cracking his gum, and 'Only eleven and so cagey. Shoulda been in school.'

'She's close to thirteen,' said Julia.

Rose had walked from window to window, immersed and hungry for things, and then strayed into the Jeans Shop.

Jean, the salesgirl at the Jeans Shop, wasn't much older than Rose, but, unlike Rose, she radiated certainty. Jean met Julia's eyes without looking away, and she must have done the same with Rose when she said, 'Can I help you?'

To Rose, a hard stare felt like a sweaty hand on her face. She looked away, hostile.

According to Jean, Rose mumbled, 'I wanna try these,' and gripped in her right hand a pair of tight jeans with light gold stitching. 'Like these.' Jean held them up to Julia.

'Change rooms are over there.' Jean had directed Rose to the back of the store, to stalls in an ordered line along the back wall. 'Rose didn't like the flimsy curtain,' said Jean. 'Most kids couldn't care less. This kid dragged the curtain closed and kept adjusting the sides, like she wanted to make certain there wasn't a gap. She dropped her jacket on the floor by the curtain, unzipped and changed her jeans, and just stood in there for a while, probably looking in the mirror. I heard her whisper "Fat." I mean, she's hardly fat, is she?'

'No,' said Julia. 'I don't think she has a mirror in her room at home.'

'Anyway, a few minutes after that, she slipped out of them, pulled on her old jeans, came out of the change stall and tried to walk past me. I said something like, "How were they?" She just looked at me and I said, "You should've come out and given us a look." But she just sort of mumbled, "Don't like them." Then she sort of roamed around, looked at some other tops, jeans and belts, touched some and studied the labels on others. Then walked back towards that first pair of jeans she'd tried, watching me out of the corner of her eye. She must have known I was suspicious. I turned away, but I could see her in the reflection here,' Jean pointed to the window. 'Rose pulled the jeans up from the table, slid them under her coat, and strolled to the door. That blonde hair makes her stand out like a beacon. Like I was stupid or something.'

'I doubt if she thought you were stupid.'

'Well, she went through the door, probably thought she was safe outside till Yashar caught her. Yashar's always polite to them.'

Yashar, an enormous young Turk in his early twenties, with dark curly hairs on the backs of his thick fingers and MECCA tattooed on the knuckles of his left hand, gripped Julia's left shoulder and said,

'Like this. I grab 'em like this. Then I'm supposed to say, "You have something you didn't pay for?"' The memory brightened his eyes. Yashar stood with his hand on Julia's shoulder, chewing and popping his gum. 'Then I says to her, "We need to see what's under your coat. Can you please come back into the store with me?" I guided her back into the store, so she wouldn't do a runner.'

He was too big for Rose to bite or punch, and too fit to run away from. Julia could see hard blue veins in chunky forearms and Atlas Security stitched on the sleeve of his tight blue shirt.

'I says to her, "Please show us what's under your jacket."' Yashar prided himself on adherence to steps. '"Nothin'," she says to me. "Nothin'." We hear that all the time – first thing out of their mouth is "nothin'", like we're stupid.'

For the second time, Julia said, 'I doubt if she thought you were stupid.'

'Then I tell 'em, "We can get the police if you like. But it'll be easier this way. Just show me what you've got under your jacket." She stood there for a while, a long while, as long she could. But I can stand there longer. When she figured that out, that I could stand there longer than she could, the kid pulled the jeans out and handed 'em over.'

'No dramas,' said Jean.

Yashar said, 'No dramas. Then Jean told her…' Yashar grinned. 'Funny name for a person working in a jeans shop – Jean.'

'Advantage when you're on a commission,' said Jean.

'Yeah, well, then Jean said to your little friend, "We'll have to call the police anyway, it's store policy." The kid flared up, called me a liar, said I'd promised not to call the police, which I never did, did I, Jean?'

'No promises,' said Jean.

'Just didn't know our store policy, that's all. Jean called the cops and I shut the door and stayed in the back room with your little friend. She didn't say a word. I says to her, '"Not real good at small talk, are ya?"' Yashar smiled. 'She sat on boxes of clothing back there lookin' mean. But we got along fine.'

Julia thought about Rose trapped in a tiny space with this hairy man between stacks of jeans and no way out. A wolf drooling over a kitten, a newborn trapped by a Rottweiler. Yashar looked like a dog in a cheap shirt except for the tattoos on his knuckles, and the waves of Brut and peppermint chewing gum coming off him.

Yashar slid his tongue along his upper lip. 'Anyway, hope you straighten her out. Not such a bad kid compared to some of the boys we get in here.' He chewed and popped his gum, tapped his foot, and drummed his fingers on a row of cardboard boxes practising his solo percussion act. 'You know, I've got my own theory about these kids.' He stood too close to Julia popping his gum, drumming his fingers and tapping his foot. Yashar seemed to be hypnotised by his drumming and forgot to tell Julia his theory.

'Yes,' said Julia, 'I'm sure you do. Thank you.'

Officer Lisa Charles had short brown hair and restless eyes in a sharp face. At the police station, she told Julia that Holly Cavanagh and Rose had waited in a dirty locked prisoner's room, the only space available. Holly's face looked hard, said Officer Charles, and guarded. She and Rose said nothing to each other, just sat on the hard metal benches in silence. There were no windows; the grey walls were covered with black scuff marks and the floor smelled like criminal's piss and Pine O Cleen.

'Can you shut me in there for a moment?' Julia said.

Lisa said, 'What?'

'Just for a short while.'

'I don't understand,' said Lisa.

'Because I don't understand this child very well. Maybe this is a start.'

'If you think it would help.'

'I do.'

Julia sat imprisoned. The smell made her want to vomit; in the shut box, she started to panic.

Lisa came and peered through a small peephole in the door. Julia heard keys jangle in the lock and watched the door swing open. They walked along a hallway lit by a line of bare light bulbs, away from the smell, the Pine O Cleen and the cinder-block room that smelled like a urinal. Lisa said she had released Holly and Rose and led them single file down this narrow, dim hallway to the interview room.

'I can understand why you might be able to counsel her better if you know what she went through, but I'm limited in what I can show you, or tell you.'

'I understand.'

'Parents sit across from us while we organise a writing pad, and check the video camera. Then the familiar, "I must caution you, Rose, that anything you say can be taken down and used as evidence against you. Do you understand that, Rose?" The girl nodded. Holly slumped in the chair over there,' she pointed, 'didn't interfere, and I asked Rose if she'd stolen anything before. Holly shook her head. A lie as it turned out. Then we say to them, "This goes on your record. If there's another incident – anything, even stealing a lolly – you go to court. Do you understand me?" Usually we get a nod out of them, and I got a small one from Rose. Then we say, "They catch a lot of people in that shop, and they'll catch you again if you go back." We say it whether it's true or not, and "If pocket money's a problem, you discuss it with your mother and father."'

'It is a problem' said Julia.

Lisa sniffed and brought her hand to her nose. 'You realise, don't you, that she'll probably do it again. I saw no remorse, no crying, and I bet she thinks nothing will happen to her. That's never good. If a kid cries a bit, there's always a better chance that she won't reoffend. Remorse, that's the key. Feeling sorry for her parents or the store owner, not themselves. She didn't even feel sorry for herself. This kid, if I'm not mistaken, will be locked up before she turns sixteen. It's not clear, at this point, what else we can do to help you, or Rose.'

Julia said, 'She was going so well, then she did this. Welfare thinks she's being interfered with by a family member.'

'That's the common element, but we can't act on rumour, and Rose has never, to my knowledge, complained to the police. Is it her father?'

'Stepfather.'

'Stepfather. Well, that's never good. Anyway, we can't do anything until someone formally complains. The complaint can be lodged by her teacher.'

'We've planned a home visit, maybe tomorrow night. And this week I'll go for a walk with Rose, see if she opens up.'

'Well, good luck. I hope she does. Give me a buzz if there's anything else we can do.'

In the car, Julia began to weep; she didn't know for whom.

17

Home Visit

Bad weather had turned on the city again. Curtains of rain hung over mountains to the west and threads of lightning cut through clouds to the east; a cold wind burst in from the river and animals over the road would soon take cover and the grass would be soaked. Mist lay heavy in the street as Brian watched Julia race down the drive and leap into her lover's car.

Kate drove out of Cook down Coulter Drive, along William Slim to Giralang, past white-pillared houses with painted black grating on the windows. White cement birdbaths sat in front yards. They coasted downhill to smaller government houses tucked in cul-de-sacs.

'Do we have a clear plan of attack?' said Kate

'To understand Lee, Holly and the kids,' said Julia.

Kate looked across at her. 'Has she stolen before?'

'She has, and she's run away from home before. We need to get Lee and Holly to a fortnightly meeting. '

'Phone them and ask.'

'I have. We got the meeting today because Holly was home alone when I phoned. Lee would have said no. He can be difficult.'

'Difficult? What do you mean difficult? Is he going to take a swing at me?'

'Probably not. But we'll see. He's more likely to listen to a big pushy woman like you than a good-natured schoolteacher like me.'

She smiled. 'Oh yeah. A woman he can identify with. A woman who loves to watch the Danish women's soccer team spank Germany in the rain, and stand in wet jerseys and hold up their trophy. The kind of woman a misogynist plumber can relate to.'

'I hope so.'

'Does he look like a plumber?'

'He combs long pieces of hair off his temples, up over his skull, then plasters them down with hair gel.'

'I can't wait.' Kate shifted down a gear as they rounded a corner. 'We'll see the family together.'

'Why not see Lee and Holly alone?'

'No, that's not how it works. Everyone together at first. Remind me of the names of the other family members.'

Julia reached across and put her hand on Kate's knee. 'Two little sisters, Debbie and Deedee, about two and four.'

'What else does Lee do with his time, besides plumb?'

'He keeps guns in the house, loves to shoot pigs, and has two Rottweilers in the backyard for hunting in the Brindabellas – one named Regal, another named Exit Wound.'

'You made that up.'

'I wish I had. The man loves Exit Wound more than his own daughters. And don't be surprised if he plays Dwight Yoakam tapes for you.'

'Dwight who?'

'Dwight Yoakam, American country singer with a voice like a high-pitched mountain holler. Lee plays Dwight when he gets angry.'

Kate hit the steering wheel with the palm of her hand, 'Dwight instead of the strap – "That's it, you kids. Settle down or I'm puttin' on the Dwight. Last warning, I mean it this time. Behave, or you're boot-scootin' to Dwight."'

'It's a given that academics hate country music.'

'Hate it? What do you mean hate it? We love it. Makes us want to jump in the pick-up and go out and kick some butt.'

'What else do you need to know?'

'I need to know if we can look forward to a good, solid hour of kick-ass country music at Lee's house tonight.'

'What else do you need to know besides that?'

'Probably a lot, but that's enough for now. One meeting a fortnight doesn't seem too much to ask for. Let's ask.'

Close to 5 p.m., they pulled up to the kerb and saw the house. The concrete drive had weeds poking up through jagged cracks. In the yard, a muddy red tricycle, a white plastic toy oven, an old grey blanket tangled in scrubby uncut grass. An opaque glass front door stood at the top of the step.

They knocked. Lee threw open the door, smiled, and acted pleased to see them. 'Come in, come in!' He swung back his arm in a welcoming arc.

They stepped in past him and Kate eyed the message on his stained T-shirt – 'Real cowboys don't line dance.'

'Lee, this is Kate.'

'Hi there.' Lee didn't shake hands, but squinted at Kate. 'Don't I know you?'

Kate stood facing him, a few centimetres taller. 'I don't think so. Maybe we've seen each other around town.'

In through the tobacco-coloured kitchen past a grey laminex table and orange vinyl chairs. Holly kept the scuffed linoleum floor clean, or maybe she'd cleaned it for their visit. An orange blind patterned with ducks above the kitchen sink covered a window that looked out on the Rottweilers.

Lee, Kate and Julia passed into the living room with its patterned blue wallpaper, the sort of decor you might find in Gracelands. Black vinyl lounge chairs sat in front of a giant seventy-centimetre Sanyo, the only sign of luxury in the room. A scuffed pine coffee table with an ashtray that looked as big as a spare tyre stood between the Sanyo and a big padded chair. Lee's for sure. On the wall hung three more ducks, and a stuffed boar's head with long tusks, Julia thought probably from Namadgi.

'Sit down, sit down,' invited Lee. 'You kids, down!' He pointed Rose and her two young sisters off the chairs, like guilty puppies.

They crawled down and sat together in front of the TV. Lee sat in the big chair, and Holly hunched in the smaller chair to his left. Debbie smiled, then crawled back up onto Lee's lap and snuggled next to him.

Julia said, 'Holly, Rose, this is Kate Selby.'

Holly nodded; the young girls looked up but Rose looked away, sitting cross-legged with her little sister under the blank Sanyo screen.

Lee smiled and petted his hair over his bald patch. He picked up a folded sheet of paper from the pine table. 'Look at this,' he demanded and tossed it on Julia's knee.

Julia unfolded the note. In neat upper case printing, it said,

> YOUR DOGS WERE BARKING ALL LAST
> NIGHT. PLEASE KEEP THEM QUIET
> OR I WILL CALL THE POLICE

He leaned towards her. 'Tryin' to stop more of our freedoms. What do you think?'

'Maybe,' Julia said, 'or maybe they're worried about the noise.'

'Twaddle. Pure claptrap. They're not that bad. Some limp-wristed bastard should have a couple beers before he goes to bed. That's all he needs. Wonder if it's a trick, someone tryin' to rob the houses around here. I bet it's a trick.' He looked away. 'Anyway, they can call anyone they like.' Lee picked up a stubby from the pine table and took a long swig. 'You're just in time.' He pressed the button on the remote.

Julia looked at the dirt under his fingernails, and in the creases of his knuckles. Glenn Bridges raced out of the wings across the giant screen as the *Make a Million* jingle blasted into the room.

'I wonder what Nicky'll be wearing tonight,' said Lee.

Nicky Bolton came swanning in, draped in a sequined dress cut low in the front, and to the waist in back. The audience cheered, Lee and Holly watched.

'Our champion is back,' beamed Glenn, 'to try for a new Holden Commodore,' the audience clapped and cheered, 'after winning a fantastic cutlery set last week.'

Lee craned forward and tapped his cigarette on the lip of the spare tyre ashtray. Holly rested back and looked hard at the television. Kate looked over at Julia, and Rose glanced up and caught her look.

'Lee,' said Kate, 'Lee, we'd like to talk about Rose.'

'Yeah, yeah, we need to, for sure. Right after this is over.'

Glenn started his questions. 'The largest ski fields are found in which country: Switzerland, France or Australia.'

'Australia! Australia!' shouted Lee. 'It's got to be Australia!'

On the television, June was too quick for the champion and pressed her button. 'Australia?' she said.

'Yes,' said Glenn, 'Australia!'

The audience roared.

Lee called out, 'I told you. Australia!'

Debbie slid down to the floor and sat next to her sisters. Lee didn't seem to notice.

Glenn again, 'This is going to be close. You're giving the champ a run for his money, June. Next question: for what film did Sylvester Stallone win the Academy Award for Best Picture?'

The champ hesitated.

'*Rocky*! *Rocky*!' shouted Lee and he leaned into the Sanyo, 'It's Rocky, you moron.'

Glenn waited, then John pressed his buzzer. 'Rambo?'

'No, sorry, John. The answer was *Rocky*.'

'I told you,' Lee shouted. '*Rocky*, I told you.' His excitement was contagious, Holly now alive to the miracle of combat.

Glenn again, 'The list of names at the end of a film describing various people's jobs in the film is called the...what?'

Lee sucked on his cigarette, looking troubled and lost.

On TV the champ pressed her buzzer. 'Credits.'

'Yes,' said Glenn, 'credits.'

The studio audience shouted and clapped.

Lee and Holly watched the Sanyo hard now, with some worry in their faces.

Glenn again, 'What is the Neil Diamond song, "Song, sung..." what?' asked Glenn. '"Song, sung..." what?'

'Blue!' yelled Lee. 'It's "Song, sung, blue", you idiot.' Lee stood up out of his black vinyl chair, yelling down at the TV.

The buzzer sounded.

'Yes, John?' asked Glenn.

'Song, sung blue,' said John.

'That's right,' said Glenn, beaming. 'That puts you in the lead!' And the audience exploded.

Kate looked again at the side of Julia's face. Julia didn't look back, thinking about the power of television to convince more than a few men they were quite smart. She sat next to Kate, watching Lee and Holly, as they perched on the edge of their chairs watching Glenn.

Julia sat looking at Rose, curled on the floor, thinking about how she needed a marmalade kitten to hold and stroke in her lap. Rose once told her that Lee wouldn't let her have a kitten, and Julia knew why. It would become an adult cat the size of a human baby, and lithe and graceful. But dogs are as dangerous as broken glass. There was a brittle ferocity in the two large dogs out back that hunted pigs in Namadgi and bellowed in Lee's backyard, and a kitten would arch in alarm if the dogs came into the house, and spit and scratch at them. Lee would toss the kitten out and let his dogs kill it. Julia ached for Rose and her emptiness, physically hurt as Rose sat in the blue and brown room with ducks and mounted pigs on the wall. Julia sat drowning in hopelessness over the lost girl before them.

Five-thirty and Glenn was finished. And so was Lee. Exhausted, coming out of his stupor, he switched off the television, looked around the room, at Holly, at Julia, at Kate. 'Right. Let's talk about Rose,' he instructed them. 'Been in trouble again, hasn't she?'

The dogs bellowed in the backyard, loud enough to shake ducks off the wall and Kate winced, but the Cavanaugh family registered nothing, as if inoculated to the barking Rottweilers or deaf from the giant Sanyo.

'The police saw me yesterday,' said Julia, 'about Rose's shoplifting incident. We can't figure out why she'd shoplift when things were going so well at school. It makes no sense.'

Kate watched Lee as he listened carefully, looking directly at Julia, squinting with a sneaky, hyena cunning.

He furrowed his brow. 'Look, ah, look, Julia, she's always been like that. A bit crazy, you know. It doesn't surprise me, or Holly. Does it, Holly?' He looked to Holly slumped in the chair.

She pushed a limp strand of hair from her forehead. There was a pause, Holly thinking about what to do, or say, then she assembled enough force to say, 'No.'

Rose sat with her head down, Holly looked back at the dead TV screen, and the two young girls moved their eyes to each adult who spoke.

'She's a wilful child,' said Lee. 'Might seem sweet to you, hoodwinks people who don't know her. But you watch. She always betrays you, shows her true colours in the end, like she did with that stealing. She'll do it again.'

Rose sat cross-legged on the floor with no expression.

Kate turned to each speaker and stroked her chin, like a detached anthropologist studying a tribe of island cannibals. She drew Lee's attention, fixed him with a comfortable stare and said. 'Can I ask you a couple of things?'

'Sure. Go ahead.'

'We're confused. It would help us if we understood, who worries most about Rose? Who's most upset when Rose gets in trouble?'

He was silent and Julia thought Lee wouldn't answer. Then he said, 'Well, Holly, I suppose.'

Kate slipped her attention from Lee to Holly. 'Can you tell me what you think about Lee's explanation for Rose's stealing, that stealing is part of her nature, that sooner or later she'll do it again?'

Holly looked up, her eyes wide. Julia knew what Kate was doing, a technique used in family therapy, and she thought it was perilous. She was pushing dangerously close to the family's secrets. Her questions built a map, showed where ties and divisions lay. The questions were meant to threaten Lee. But why would Kate do this?

There'd been silence in the room while everyone looked at Holly and waited. Rose, her slight body curled on the floor, waited.

Lee sat back in his king-sized chair and crossed his arms over his chest. 'This is a waste of time,' he said. 'The kid needs a firmer hand. She'll get it this time.'

Holly said, 'I think Rose is asking for help.'

The room went quiet. Lee turned red, his mouth set.

Kate turned to Rose on the floor. 'We seem to have a difference of opinion here, Rose. What do you think about your mother's explanations for your stealing?'

Rose kept her eyes down, avoided the gaze of people watching her in the room, her face white as aspirin. 'Don't know.' She reddened and narrowed her eyes. She resented Kate's intrusion.

Kate probed, switched attention from Holly to Rose and Lee and back again; she controlled the show. 'Holly, you said Rose was trying to get help. Help for what?'

Lee's mouth opened slightly as he realised the questions were full of traps. His eyes widened. 'Always conning people for sympathy.'

Kate ignored him, cut him off from his family again. 'What do you think, Holly?'

She paused and cleared her throat. More hesitation, then she said, 'Rose isn't happy.' There was a touch of heartache in her voice, a lilt.

'Any chance we could meet every couple of weeks and sort this out?'

Lee's arms suddenly unfolded like springs, as if he suddenly realised there were two big egos in the room and one had to stand up and spray its territory. He banged his hands on his knees, leaned forward in his chair and stood. 'It's late. I think Holly and Rose don't like this much. We better get these kids some dinner. I have to get up early and work. We're not schoolteachers.'

In the quiet blue foil room, he stood looking at the floor, dismissive, bored and arrogant. Lee, the man of the house, would protect his family. His pupils lay wide and black.

'Okay, Lee,' said Kate, 'Can we meet in a fortnight?'

'We'll see,' said Lee. That meant, 'No way.' The anger in Lee almost erupted, almost looked like courage. He reached down to his stereo unit and clicked the On button. Out of the speakers came a maudlin nasal Tennessee voice, a high-pitched mountain holler – 'Two doors down, there's a barmaid that serves 'em real strong, here lately that's how I make it through… Two doors down there's a bar stool that knows me by name, we sit there, together and wait for you…'

Julia stood and waited. The family ignored her. 'Well, thank you, we appreciate your time.'

The family sat wordless. Holly looked harassed and frightened as Lee stared past Kate and Julia. He watched them file out of the living room, back through the orange-grey kitchen to the opaque glass front door. Kate twisted the metal lock. The porch light was off, or broken. They stepped into the night over the muddy toy oven, shut the door behind them, moved along the driveway to Kate's car. The Rottweilers boomed at them through the fence.

They climbed into the Volvo, Kate started it and backed out of the driveway. Julia could hear muffled steel guitar, and Dwight wailing about something sad. In the corner of the window, a thin white hand pulled the curtain aside. Julia couldn't see who spied on them.

Rain slammed down; they hissed over Giralang streets.

Julia leaned against the passenger-side door and listened to Kate pour out scorn, jerking the car around corners, speaking with a hard uncontrolled rage. 'If the cops don't stop him, I'll stop him.'

'Why are you so upset? You cut Lee off from his family. What were you thinking? You knew he'd show you the door.'

'He's a coward, a bastard.'

Julia reached across the seat and touched her. 'What's this about?'

'Men who lie, men who hurt children.'

'You're not handling this very well.'

Kate skidded the Volvo around a wet corner. 'You're not getting anywhere with him.'

'Why take it so personally? Forget about Lee for now.'

Red tail lights floated ahead of them, bloody spots in the rain.

Neither spoke as Kate steered the Volvo through Kaleen to the traffic lights on Belconnen Way. She hit the brakes like she was crushing a cockroach underfoot, skidded the car sideways in the rain. Kate backed up the car, straightened it and drove through when the light turned green.

Julia gave her a few minutes, waited for her to calm before she said, 'Kate?'

'What.'

'How would you describe that house?'

Kate thought for a moment. 'Subtle.'

'I would say, delicate.'

'Restrained. Understated. I loved the orange in the kitchen, and how the blue aluminium foil tastefully reflected Glenn Bridges on Sonya.'

'The family was good at *Make a Million*.'

Kate nodded. 'Really good. They're a nice couple. I love to see one couple sharing a brain.'

Julia was quiet. 'Can I make a suggestion?'

'Sure.'

'Let's go to Wattle Street?'

'Sure. You got a key?'

'I do.'

Julia felt Kate's body loosen and rest back in the seat. They drove through O'Connor towards the school and Kate said, 'There's one important thing we learned.'

'What's that?'

'How to get Lee to these meetings.'

'How?'

'Free set of steak knives.'

'You sure?'

'Positive.'

Kate pulled the car into Wattle Street and switched off the ignition.

18

Admission

'For if they fall, the one will lift up his fellow;
but woe to him that is alone when he falleth;
for he hath not another to help him.'

Rain whispered on the roof. Julia woke and readied for school. She drove along Macarthur Avenue and watched the morning clear to a polished blue over steamy streets.

Rose sat cross-legged on a blanket on damp grass outside Jeremy's office. The eagle lay prone and weak on bedding of old sheets and they had expected Jeremy to arrive one morning without her. But the eagle remained with them, arrived in her basket each day, maybe staying alive for Rose.

The eagle had changed. Longer brown feathers poked through white down on the trailing edge of each wing. Dark feathers had emerged on her back. She sat up in the basket, her jet-black eyes watched her own powdery down float away on updraughts, and stick to high branches in wattles and eucalypts at the edge of the schoolyard. She watched birds, often turning her head upside down to gain perspective, then turning it back again. With mistrust, she eyed anybody who came close to the basket, except Rose.

Jeremy medicated the eagle and never stopped teaching. 'This is oxytetracycline,' he said to Rose, 'a broad spectrum antibiotic. But each capsule has two hundred and fifty milligrams and I'll give her three. Each capsule has about as much as you would give to an Alsatian dog.'

'Why so much?'

'Because birds operate differently to mammals, so they need much higher doses. We don't know what's wrong with her, so we'll try this for a week. No longer.'

A few weeks before, Jeremy had organised a puppet, a cardboard cut-out of an eagle's head that he folded over a pair of tweezers. He told Rose that, from that day on, she needed to use the puppet when she fed the eagle. 'Eventually, you'll have to disguise yourself under a big coat.'

As Jeremy and Julia watched, Rose picked red slivers of meat from a saucer, and held them to the eagle's open beak with the tweezers folded under the puppet head. The eagle grabbed each piece and, flipping her head backwards, threw the meat into the back of her mouth and pulled it into her throat with a hook on the back of her tongue. She swallowed each piece whole, and gave a chirping call as she ate, a delicate sound from such a powerful animal.

Jeremy had said to Julia, 'The cardboard puppet will stop the eagle from recognising humans as her parents. If she grows up to see humans as her parents, she'll attack them after she can fly.'

'Attack them?' said Julia.

'Because she'll start to attack her parents at that stage.'

'Seems strange.'

'They harass their parents, chase after them for food, or sometimes play a little rough. Male eagles are smaller than their daughters, so they don't like it. Eventually, the males fly in, drop prey near the nest, and speed off before their sons or daughters can grapple with them and tear the food away.'

'They're frightened of their own adolescent offspring?'

'Their offspring are as large as they are. It's just the way young eagles are socialised.'

Rose, on the ground outside Jeremy's open window, heard them talking, but she didn't look up. She isolated herself in a small world with no people, leaning over the basket, rocking herself back and forth on the grass as she spoke to the eagle. The eagle, lying in shade, continued the high, sweet piping as her eyes fluttered shut.

Julia leaned out of Jeremy's window and whispered, 'Rose.'

She looked up. 'Yeah.'

'Let's go to my place for some lunch. Ruth can take the boys, Jeremy can watch the eagle. They'll be fine.'

Rose grimaced. 'What for?'

'Come on. Let's get out of this place.'

She stood, paused and looked into the basket. The eagle breathed deeply now, eyes shut, in sleep. Rose came inside, washed her hands, retrieved her exercise book from her desk, and came out to face Julia.

Julia started towards the door and reached her hand back, her fingers motioning, 'Come on. Let's go.'

They strolled down the corridor into the parking lot.

In the car, Rose twisted the dials on the radio, looking for music, but said very little on the way. In ten minutes, they reached Cook. After they pulled into the driveway, she got out and squatted to pat Bonnie and talk to her, face to face, before Julia motioned her in through the front door.

'Make yourself at home, Rose. I'll make some sandwiches. What would you like?'

'Anything.' She sat at the table, rigid and suspicious.

Julia decided to wait until after lunch to ask her about Lee. As they ate, Rose talked about Bonnie, and about taking the eagle to the river nest.

The hour went. She mixed excitement with some lament, and Julia let Rose lead the talk. With her hands, she made shapes, often talking with her mouth full.

They left the house and Rose knelt and held Bonnie's face in her hands and talked with her until Julia said they had to go.

Sitting in the passenger seat on the way back to school, she wrote in the exercise book and Julia watched traffic and didn't snoop.

They arrived at the school parking lot with fifteen minutes to themselves before the end of lunch.

Julia said, 'Let's go for a walk to Haig Park.'

'What for?'

'Just come.' And Julia led her out of the schoolyard, down the cement path towards the park.

A gentle wind drifted through the tops of pines against blue sky, needles and sap oozing from rough trunks, sharp in their noses, as if the park had just been disinfected.

Rose walked by her side, sometimes bumping Julia's arm with her shoulder, but she walked in silence. She watched a man in front of them with a blue heeler. The man followed the dog to a rough pine trunk and waited as the dog lifted its leg.

Julia stopped by an oleander bush. 'Just about everything on this tree is poison. Any oleanders at your place?'

'Don't know.'

They walked further and Julia knew Rose anticipated something bad. 'Rose, you know we all like you. Ruth and Jeremy think the world of you, and they say in meetings that you make the unit a better place.'

They walked, and Rose's fists tightened a little.

'But there's something going on that doesn't add up. We've worked with children for a long time, and when girls start to go...well, get into trouble, like you have, there's normally a good reason for it. Girls don't go out and steal from shops and get in trouble with the police for no reason.'

Rose's honey-blonde hair drifted in the wind.

'Has anything happened at home, or at school?'

She walked silently at Julia's side with her head down. She seemed to be drifting away.

'Can you talk to me about home? Is there trouble?'

She walked on, silent, her face hard.

'I know you're a loyal person, that you don't want to dob on anyone. But there's something going on.'

She moved further from Julia, reached up to scratch her nose.

Julia thought, maybe she can't speak. 'Rose, you've got to help us. There is something going on, isn't there? Is it Lee?'

No response, and it felt perilous now. Hair on the back of Julia's neck bristled.

Kate would later say that Julia hadn't been neutral, and Julia would respond, 'You're hardly neutral, are you?' Kate replied, 'You should have used open-ended questions at first,' and Julia would say, 'Screw the open-ended questions. We're talking about Lee.'

Rose and Julia strolled quietly for a time, shoes scuffing on grass and dirt, sun cutting through gaps in the pine limbs.

After a long two or three minutes, Julia asked again, 'Help me, Rose. Is it someone at school, or at home?'

Rose shook her head. 'Leave me alone.'

'Just let me help you.'

Both standing quiet, facing each other on the path.

'It's Lee, isn't it?'

Quiet except for traffic hissing down Northbourne Avenue.

Julia was driven and frightened and angry. She didn't know if persistence would pay off, or maybe land her in the dock with Lee's solicitor grilling her over the exact words she'd used that afternoon to pry falsehoods out of Rose. She decided to abandon this harangue, leave Rose alone. But then it was too clear, the answer to Rose's suffering, the secret muttered behind glass doors in her house, the whispering catastrophe that drove her to steal and set fires and fight teachers. It lay just beyond her reach, and Julia fell just short of kicking it, and kicking Lee's smirking face and killing the evil inside the house in Giralang.

'Rose, I have to keep asking…'

'Leave us alone.'

'Rose, I…'

She turned and shouted, 'Are you deaf?'

'Rose.'

Shouting at the ground. 'No.'

'Rose, try to understand –'

'Okay!' she turned and shouted in her face. 'Okay!'

'Okay what?' Julia felt some relief, as if she'd broken through and won the first victory in a battle to destroy Lee. 'Rose, you have to tell me what's going on.'

They walked through the park, sandals slapping on the wooden bridge over the creek, then cut east along Condamine Street.

Silent, Rose stopped and turned away from a car rushing by; she started back. Five minutes, maybe ten minutes of silent meandering with Julia following her on the dirt path until the school came into view, a hundred metres time to break Lee's grip. A cold wind scuttled papers along the gutter and rippled Julia's dress. They stopped and stood together looking at the school over the road. Julia knew she had bungled her attempt to beat Lee, and she felt sick over it.

Then Rose said, 'Yes.'

'Yes what, Rose?'

'Yes.' There was crying in her voice.

'What does he do?'

She wagged her head slowly.

'What does he do?'

'He'll kill me and my sisters if I tell.'

'Does he have intercourse with you?'

'No.'

'Have you told your mother?'

'It happens when she's gone, like in hospital.'

'You told her?'

'She doesn't do anything. They fight about it.'

'Your mother and Lee fight about it?'

Rose stood without speaking and looked at the school.

'We have to talk to the police, Rose, or to Welfare. We have to get help for you and your sisters.'

'No.' She turned and raised a fist. 'No.'

'Rose, we have to.'

'No.' Lips tight against her teeth. 'If you tell anyone, I'll say you're lying.'

'Rose…'

'Leave us alone.'

'Rose, we have to stop him.'

'It won't happen.'

'Rose…'

'If you tell anyone, I'll say it was you doing it. Or Jeremy in his office.'

Julia stopped. Rose walked a few steps into the schoolyard. Julia caught up with her, grabbed her arm and spun her around, tried to force her to look, but Rose stared past her.

'Can I talk to your mother, then? Can I tell her what we talked about today? You just said already she knows.'

'Stay away from my house.'

'Let me talk to her. I won't tell her what you said.'

'Stay away from us.' She looked at the ground with her arms folded.

'If you won't let me talk to your mother, I have to talk to the police.' More than a little extortion in her tone.

Silence for a time.

Then Rose looked up from the ground. 'All right.'

'I can talk to her?'

Rose stared past Julia.

'You get on the bus at the end of school today. I'll talk to your mother and leave the house before you get home.'

They walked through the heavy glass and metal doors into the grey hallway, down to Jeremy's office.

'Jeremy, can I ask a favour?'

'Sure.' He looked at Rose standing next to her.

'Phone Rose's mother and ask her if I can pop around to see her this afternoon.'

'Sure, I can do that.'

19

Visiting Holly

'Women can't forgive failure.'

Julia pulled into the Cavanaughs' front drive. The same broken toys on scrubby grass and burnt patches on the lawn. Curtains shut tight at four in the afternoon. Climbing up to the opaque glass door, she knocked and heard no sound from inside. She knocked three more times.

She turned to walk back down the steps then heard the metallic clink of the lock and the door opened on squeaky hinges. She turned to face Holly. 'I didn't know if you were home or not.'

'Yeah. Come in.' She squinted from the glare outside, and gave Julia a troubled smile. Barefoot in a terry-towel robe, she escaped back into the dark.

Julia stepped in and closed the door, followed Holly into the tobacco-coloured kitchen, where Holly motioned her to sit at the table.

With difficulty, she looked up, like a shy child. 'Want some coffee?'

'That would be good.'

Holly reached into the cupboard for a jar of instant and two brown cups.

'Thanks for agreeing to see me,' said Julia. 'We've been concerned about Rose. Seems you are too.'

'Yeah.'

Julia watched Holly unscrew the lid off the coffee. 'We can't understand why she'd go down to the mall and steal when everything was going so well. Jeremy says she's gifted with animals, and her schoolwork is good. Why do you think she missed school?'

Holly stood quietly in her towelling bathrobe, looking at the linoleum floor; Julia waited a long minute in the orange-grey silence. Talking to Holly, she decided, was like talking to Rose.

One of the dogs bellowed in the backyard.

'I had a long talk with Rose today. She had lunch at my house, then walked with me to Haig Park. She told me there'd been some trouble. Can you tell me about it?'

Holly kept her gaze to the floor, dead quiet, she rubbed her fist under her nose, then rubbed her eye.

Julia reached into her pocket. 'Here's a tissue.'

Holly took the tissue, wiped her nose and eyes. She sank into the chair, and twisted the tissue into a rope on her lap. 'Lee's been worried about the dogs.'

'Dogs?'

'Yeah.'

'The letter, you mean?'

'Someone's angry about the barking, but it could be somebody else.'

'Other pig hunters?'

'Maybe. Maybe neighbours.'

'They're a bit loud, aren't they?'

'The dogs?'

'Yes.'

'After someone put the threat letters in the mailbox, a guy came to the door and got in a fight with Lee.'

'About the dogs?'

'Yeah. And Lee says they're just trying to keep the dogs quiet around here so they can rob houses.'

'They probably wouldn't come to your door and complain if that was the case.'

'He says it's the same people trying to take our guns away, so we can't protect ourselves.' Holly leaned her elbows on the table, slumped forward in the chair.

'These are the same people complaining about the dogs?'

'Somebody threw snail bait over the fence.'

'Snail bait? I don't understand.'

'It poisons dogs. Made Regal sick, but not Exit. A hundred and four dollars so far at the vet. Regal's still there. Rose was pretty upset, and Lee sort of took it out on her.'

'Took it out on Rose? What does Rose have to do with Regal being poisoned?'

'He just does that. Says she's not his kid, says she makes trouble.'

Though Julia was listening carefully, she was lost, helpless. 'How can we stop Lee from hurting Rose?'

Holly looked away and pressed her lips together. There was a long silence. 'He's not sure Rose didn't poison them. Nothing I can do about it, I'm just spare change around here. I can't say much.' Slumped in her chair, twisting the tissue tight now, she looked tired and old.

'It must be very hard.'

'It's harder now, with all this dog business.' She fingered the collar on her bathrobe.

'Why would he think Rose did it?'

'Could be other pig-doggers that're jealous of Lee, or could be the rangers. The rangers hate him.'

They sat at the kitchen table. Neither of them spoke. Either she had no idea of what Julia was asking, or she did know and wanted to deflect their discussion away from Rose onto the dogs. Or maybe she was talking in code and Julia was too obtuse to understand it. She hadn't made the coffee and she never did.

'Holly, Rose told me there were things going on with Lee.'

She sat looking down and chewing her bottom lip. 'It's true.'

'Holly, we need to do something about it. Do you have any ideas?'

Silence, then she said, 'I was young.'

'When you had Rose?'

'Rose was only three when I met him, and a good baby, always smiling. But I couldn't raise her on my own.'

Julia nodded.

'I met him at my brother's place, they used to be mates, working on cars, playing with guns. He'd just come down from Bathurst.'

'Your brother's from Bathurst?'

'And Lee's from Bathurst. I am too. He was kind then, Lee was. He bought me things, bought presents for Rose, and I thought he'd be good to us. He said he would. We needed somebody to take care of us.'

'Then he changed?'

'Maybe he'll change back.'

'He might change back, Holly, but how can we help Rose?'

A pause, then she said, 'Debbie and Deedee love him.'

'One thing we could do, Holly, is to ask Dr Barnardo's if they'd take her in at Downer, or into their foster parents program. Get her out of this house long enough to figure out what to do.'

No reply.

'Holly, that should make Lee happy. He shouldn't object. We need to look after Rose. I think you know that.'

'You have to leave us alone.' She pushed a strand of brown hair off her face and tucked it behind one ear.

'What?'

'You have to go away.'

'Holly, if we get Rose into Barnardo's, we aren't blaming Lee, or blaming anyone. In our recommendation, we link it to her stealing.'

'He'll hurt someone.'

'Holly, we have to do something in the long term about Rose.'

She shook her head. 'Not now.'

'But you have to…'

Julia heard the rattle of keys and the clink of the lock in the glass front door. It squeaked and she thought she heard Rose coming in. But Holly raised her face towards the door, pupils wide and black, skin on her hands as white as the tissue she had crumpled in her fist. The door slammed and she tried to stand, but trembled and fell back down.

Heavy shoes clomped down the hallway, the kitchen door swung open.

'Hey, Julia,' in his high, yammering voice. Lee stalked into the kitchen, long strides, wearing stained overalls that smelled like faeces.

The room grew smaller. He threw his keys and they clattered on the kitchen bench. He swaggered past the two women seated at his table, pulled open the fridge door and took out a stubby, twisted the top off and hopped onto the kitchen bench. He looked down at them for a moment, tipped his head back and took a long swig. 'Go ahead, go ahead. Don't let me interrupt.' He ran his finger in a circle around his damp lips.

Holly looked at the floor, her white hands quivering.

'Holly was just telling me about Regal. That's bad news.'

'Yeah, it is. I'll catch the bastard that did it.'

'Are the police involved?'

'Police?' His head lolled back in a twittering chuckle. 'As someone said in a song once, "The cops don't need you and man they expect the same." But yeah, I told 'em.'

Holly sat with her head down, fingering the belt on her robe.

'I hope they catch them,' said Julia.

'Do you now? And what if "them" is your little friend Rose? What then? Hope the police catch Rose?'

'You think Rose would poison a dog?'

'I know she would. You don't know what you're dealing with.'

'We're trying to understand why she's had this rough patch.'

Lee tipped his head back, swigged his beer in long slurpy gulps, sitting above them while Julia looked up and waited. He belched, neck bristled with rusty brown stubble. He clunked the bottle on the kitchen bench and squinted. 'I told you. That's just the way she is. She cons teachers first, because they're easiest. But sooner or later they see the light, or the darkness.'

'Incidentally, it's good to see you here. I thought you worked until six each day.'

He lit a cigarette and paused, blew smoke into the room and watched it eddy near the ceiling. 'I do. But I saw your car and thought

I'd drop in. Got to push off in a minute. Another job.' His eyes dropped into a sleepy sort of cunning.

Julia smiled back. 'I'm glad you could make it. Can I ask, Lee, do you think Rose's problems have anything to do with you?'

It was a clumsy move and she knew it. But she wanted to punch his buttons; she'd grown tired of holding back around Lee and wanted to defy his in-house authority. She wanted her lack of submission to enrage him.

His neck flared red at the collar. He took another long swig of beer, looked out the window, then down at Julia. 'Anything to do with me? What do you mean me? Think, schoolteacher.' His eyes flashed white against his red face, and Julia thought he wanted to grab her and put her head through the glass front door. 'What would you people know? Huh? What the fuck would you know? She doesn't steal from me, you morons. She stole from the mall when she's supposed to be at fuckin' school, in your care.'

A thin rail of smoke rose from his cigarette. He jerked the bottle from the bench, spilled some of it foaming over his knee, stuck it into his bristly face, gulping with his eyes to the ceiling. He tucked the bottle tight in his crotch. An oily strand of hair fell over his eyebrow. He reached up and smoothed it back.

'Lee, we're going to have to involve Welfare, maybe the police. Do you understand?'

She knew full well how Lee would react to 'Do you understand?,' and she felt some warmth about it.

'What do you mean, "Do I understand?"' He stared now, leaned closer. 'Do I *what*?'

Calm as a Labrador, she sat at his kitchen table smiling up at him. 'Rose has some difficulties and she needs more help. That's what I mean.'

'I'll tell you what you fucking mean,' he pointed the neck of the bottle down at her, 'and you'll fuckin' well listen. You people are meddling in my family. You can't fix her up, so you blame me and

Holly. That's what you fuckin' mean.' He was ferocious now to Julia's indifference.

Julia nodded and smiled and he looked as though he would leap off the bench. 'Lee, we think Rose should go to Barnardo's.'

He leapt down and started towards her. Julia felt like standing up, but she stayed put with him looming over her. He blew rancid hop fumes in her face. He glared down, the bottle raised over his head, fighting evil at his table; the selfless bloke standing guard over his helpless wife and kids, the honest working man standing alone against moral turpitude.

Then he spun away from Julia. 'We need some music in here,' and rushed into the sitting room.

Julia heard the knob click on the stereo and the voice of Dwight Yoakam. 'Two doors down, there's a barmaid, who makes them real strong, Sometimes lately, that's how I make it through...'

Lee marched in heavy strides to the kitchen, threw himself back up onto the bench and looked out the window into the backyard and the remaining dog lying on a burnt patch of grass.

'Sorry you feel that way Lee. Anyway, we'll be in touch.'

'Your friend Dr Selby is conning you. She knows more than she lets on.'

Julia sat for a moment, glanced away, then stood and looked at him sitting on the bench, and at Holly sitting with her head down. 'Thanks, Holly.' She turned and walked into the hallway, winced at the squeak in the front door. She was accustomed now to letting herself out of the Cavanaugh house. She closed the door behind her, and walked to her car.

She cranked the window down and from the Mazda she could hear muffled yelling inside the house and Dwight Yoakam singing. She sat with the window down, and listened to Lee shouting croaky abuse at Holly. Julia guessed the words he spat in her face.

She hit the ignition and used the time driving home to think about what she'd done.

20

Leaving

At the heart of evolution lies the death of babies. For
natural selection to work, babies need to die, the offspring
of unfit parents. Hopefully more of yours than mine.

Julia dreamed about Lee's father, John Cavanaugh, the dignified school
inspector in a beef-coloured jacket with leather patches at the elbows,
and knife-like creases in his trousers. Orange flames from the campfire
danced in the shine off his black shoes as he stamped his foot print all
over Lee, and cast Lee into a pile of pig shit. Lee crawled out and rested
his rifle on the scattered body parts of seven pigs with cut-off ears that
were cooking in the campfire coals. Seven pairs of pig ears laid in a neat
row on a log.

'Proud of me, Dad?' said Lee. 'This is the way we do things down
south in Canberra, that fine, shiny little town, all that land to run the
dogs.'

Handing his dad a pair of bloody sliced-off women's ears on a
string, Lee told him, 'Show the family up in Bathurst, Dad, show 'em
how we do things down in the big smoke. Give a pair to the missus.'

Julia told Kate over the phone about her walk in the park with Rose,
and her second visit to Lee's house, but Kate seemed uninterested. Julia
asked if she had learned any more about Lee in Bathurst and Kate was
subdued, distracted.

'Look, I have a lot on my mind at the moment. I'll phone Mum
and find out what I can, and bring it to Thursday's meeting.'

But during the meeting Kate added little about Lee's father, the school inspector, or Lee's brilliance in the classroom, the events that led him to the style of civil disobedience he had adopted and stuck to. Wattle Street had no better understanding of Lee or the stepdaughter in their care than they had on the day she first came.

On the trail up Black Mountain, Kate looked better, though her eyes were red and cast down, her wide shoulders collapsed inwards. On a farm dam below them, a dozen fairy martins hunted with grace. Their crescent shadows flickered over the pond as they stooped over the glassy surface, and touched the water in long clean slices. A cultivated strap of dark green lay over the parkway to the south, a cork plantation that, from above, looked like crowded broccoli heads.

They climbed high enough to see west over Mount Painter, and to the Brindabellas, free to drift along the rim. Kate stood next to Julia in the spring sun, then she walked ahead with dilemmas drifting through her head.

On the mountain in clean light, Julia watched her. 'You seem upset today.'

'Let's not talk about it.' Finally she turned back and asked Julia, 'How are things at your place?'

'My place?'

'Yes.'

'A silent war of attrition during the day, then sleeping in the same bed at night. I touch him by accident, and curl back into myself. Is that what you wanted to hear?'

Kate put her arm around Julia's shoulder. 'And the kids?'

'Not good. It's a mess, and I see no way out. Yet another failure. My own family.'

Kate listened. 'You should blame me.'

Julia said, 'My father used to say, "Really beautiful things always make me cry." He used to cry when he watched *Casablanca*. The last year I was at home, he'd retired from the post office and had that dead look in his eyes that you see in old men who used to be powerful. He was confused and uncertain. And like most sentimental men he was cruel.'

Kate walked by her side and looked ahead. 'Then Brian came along.'

'Brian's father was the opposite of mine. He was kind but spineless, dominated by a large troll of a woman, a bat full of poison. I hated visiting their house. Brian's father never stood up to her, even when she mistakenly blamed Brian for dropping a bottle of jam in the kitchen. He was only ten, and his mother ordered his father to beat him, and his father did. Brian never forgave him, and I know what Brian's thinking right now: "Did I marry my bitch mother?"'

'I doubt if he thinks that.'

'I've turned into a monster.'

Kate walked beside her as she poured out her sorrow. They rounded the top of the hill and saw Mount Franklin capped in white.

'Late snow,' said Kate.

They looked at it for a moment.

'Why do we come here?'

Julia said, 'That should be obvious. It's sinful, and dangerous, and we have no choice.'

'Maybe.'

'No maybe about it.'

'I have this recurring dream,' said Julia. 'I'm at a party, tied to a tree in a powder-blue dress, and these boys are shooting arrows at me. One nicks the inside of my thigh and they come and lift up my dress to see how badly I'm cut. In the dream, the sensation is so erotic that I go home and have the first orgasm I've had for months.'

Kate shook her head. 'Too dark for me. I can't begin to understand what that means.'

They drifted further uphill and reached the native cherry, their turnip-shaped dome, and she pulled Julia by the hand under low fronds. In shade, hidden by the latticework of green, they lay next to each other looking up. Wedges of blue leaked through. When Julia looked over, Kate had closed her eyes.

She said, without opening them, 'It's probably unwise to park your car at the end of my street and walk to my place any more. The neighbours. Phone me and I'll come and pick you up somewhere, maybe in Jamison.'

'Fine.'

She pointed at the lattice roof over them. 'You know these are parasites.'

'What do you mean?'

'Native cherries parasitise other trees. Put their roots down, and tap into the roots of other trees, steal their food and kill them.'

'What's your point?'

She lay there, quiet. 'I have no point. I've been sleeping badly so I wander at night, along streets, and paths between houses, sometimes into the city. Thinking about things.'

'I'm sorry.'

'Last Friday night, I was sitting at home, alone. It hurt too much, so I walked to Belconnen Mall, to be among strangers. Plenty of time and no direction. Lost and making good time.'

'You walked there?'

'I trudged past the small shops on the second level, past couples looking in windows, kids with their arms around each other. When you're alone, you watch lovers, like a force against cold isolation. I wandered to the other side of the centre and saw this tiny Asian girl, three or four years old, like a brown enamelled doll. She trailed behind this stern, solid woman with greying hair, ruddy and Celtic, reminded me of Ruth, so the child must have been adopted, or fostered.

'In the linen section of Grace Brothers, she followed as this woman sorted through piles of sale linen set up on tables, looking for a bargain. It probably doesn't make any sense now, but I couldn't stop watching them, I don't understand it myself. It was a strange sight, this ceramic doll following a rough country woman. The woman spoke to the salesgirl in a hard country voice, and she, the woman, ignored the little girl who stood at her back. The girl trailed after her, then stopped and stood in the middle of the aisle. The woman played a cruel game with her, walked away and disappeared down the aisle. The child followed her like an imprinted duck.

'She started to cry in this tiny, piping voice, "Mummy, Mummy," and it cut me. That bitch, that coarse, grey woman just walked away. Teaching the girl a lesson. She left the little girl behind, until, finally, the girl ran after her crying, "Mummy, don't leave me." She stamped her little feet and began to cry again.

'I stood in the aisle and watched the little girl. She had this sleek black hair, like she'd been licked by a mother cat, and I decided to pick her up, you know, protect her. Then I knew I was going to do it, I couldn't be stopped. I walked over to pick her up and hold her. She continued to cry as she followed the surrogate mother around, the mother acting like she wanted to ditch her, threading her way between tables, then out the door.

'The little girl ran after her and I followed them. But her sobbing drifted off, and they disappeared. Then I noticed a young couple, maybe twenty years old, holding each other and walking and looking in shop windows. The couple passed by and looked at me. I looked back, and the girl with her arm around her friend leaned over and whispered something to her. They both stood and looked at me.

'Then for the first time in weeks, I looked at my reflection in the window. I don't look in mirrors any more, but I looked in the display window of Grace Brothers. The damage is obvious, isn't it? Everyone must know. Maybe I'm vain, but I'm female, and it's so obvious. I'm getting old. I turned away from the window and walked home, undressed, and fell asleep.

'At two that morning, the sheets were damp under me, and the doona lay strewn on the floor. I woke up sweating because it dawned on me, in my sleep, that I will never have a family. And more. I realised that I wanted to take that little girl. If I'd picked her up and walked away, I'd be finished. Nobody, not a soul except you would understand. I'd be done for.

'I fell asleep again, but about 3 a.m. I sat bolt upright in bed, straight out of my sleep, and looked around. Somewhere in the room a child had called out, "Kate."'

Kate was quiet again. After five minutes or so, she lay asleep, facing away from Julia.

On the soft bed of grass, Julia folded herself against the curve of her back and warmed her. Kate's breathing was deep and even and was the only sound Julia heard except rustling in the trees.

After ten minutes, Kate jerked her eyes open, turned over and put her hand on Julia's stomach. 'We'd better go.'

They rolled out from under the tree into coppery light. The afternoon had cooled.

Julia picked leaves and twigs from Kate's hair, and Julia wanted to talk, but Kate didn't speak as Julia followed her down the mountain.

21

Lee's Threats

Adolescent ravens at carcasses yell to bring in other young ravens, show their know-how at finding food and giving it away. A female might consider this quality of showing off when her time comes to choose a mate.

Jeremy continued to come in, wave his arms around, and talk about nature-based schemes that would save hopeless boys in his care. Julia tried to listen patiently, then turned and walked out of the school. She was tired in the afternoon, disappointed that Jeremy failed to understand how bad luck at Wattle Street came and went as it pleased. It had an agenda of its own, and returned that week for a long visit.

At home, two days after the failed interview with Holly and Lee, she sat with Ben, together in the quiet night. Brian stayed at school in a teachers' meeting until ten.

The phone rang, they jumped a little, and Ben said, 'I'll get it.' He reached over and grabbed the receiver. 'Hello, this is Benjamin Honeychurch speaking.' He waited. 'Hello.' And waited again. 'Mum, there's nobody there.'

Julia looked up from her book. They had received five or six dead phone calls yesterday, and that was the fourth call tonight. She stood and walked to the phone. 'Hello. Who's there?'

No response.

'Look, this isn't funny. If it happens again, whoever you are, I'll call the police.' Julia hung up.

'Come on, Ben, finish your reading. We'll get you into the bath.'

Five minutes later, the phone rang.

'Leave it, Ben. Just leave it.'

The phone kept buzzing, one minute, two minutes of racket, once every second like water dripping in a metal sink. Julia rushed over, picked it up and said nothing. Only static at first.

She waited then gave a controlled, dignified, 'Hello.'

Deep breathing on the other end of the line.

'All right, Lee,' said Julia. 'This is for the police to sort out,' and she banged down the receiver. She pointed. 'Ben, in the bath.'

'Who's Lee?'

'We can talk about it tomorrow.' Julia rushed around the house picking up clothes and toys, anything. 'In the bath. Let's go.'

An hour later, with the kids in bed, Julia heard Bonnie crying and barking in the front yard. She growled and barked for some five minutes and Julia knew Lee was standing outside watching the house. From her barking, Julia tried to gauge his location in the yard. He seemed be moving to the side of the house, under her bedroom window.

She walked around and checked all the locks and windows; she switched on the answering machine and sat in the lounge room and waited.

When Bonnie settled, Julia took off her clothes, put on a long T-shirt and climbed into bed. It warmed her and she let her body go limp.

A crash. It sounded like it was inside. Julia leapt from bed, covered herself in a robe and listened. Another bang from the porch.

Julia opened the door and rushed to Ben's room, then to Claire's. Asleep, breathing deeply. Julia padded into the kitchen, stood and listened. It was still, and Bonnie was quiet. She wondered if Lee had poisoned Bonnie in retribution.

She peered out the kitchen window into the backyard, then switched on the porch light. She expected Lee's face to loom out of the night and press against the window. Crippled by stories of women alone in houses with evil men stalking them, she crouched on the floor and waited, heart thumping in her ears. He didn't come.

She stood again and peered through the back window. In the porch light, a possum sat on the railing. As Julia tried to look past the animal for Lee in the corner of the yard, skulking behind a wall, the possum raised itself, balanced on its hind legs and brushed its nose with one paw. It looked in the window at her.

Julia shone a torch through the window into the backyard. He must be there. Her deep, fast breathing made her light-headed, and a little sick. The circle of the torch beam raced around the backyard and searched for Lee. Nothing. She switched off the torch and waited.

After fifteen minutes, she switched off the porch light, walked into the sitting room and decided to phone Kate. She'd committed the number to memory so Brian wouldn't find it written on a slip of paper in a book or in her bag and tackle her. She had learned in the past year to be thorough about deceit, living each day behind razor wire in a camp ruled by an occupying enemy.

She punched in Kate's numbers and waited. The phone burred, once, twice, three times. The phone must have been turned off, she thought, or maybe Kate was out. Maybe she'd gone walking. Frightened, and desperate now to speak with Kate.

Kate's phone beeped three more times. 'Hello,' in her burly voice.

'It's me. Can you talk?'

'Of course. I'm glad you called.'

'How are you feeling?'

'Don't worry about me.'

'Tell me how things are.'

'I feel like diving off a high building.'

'I'm sorry, darling. I wish I could come over.'

'I wish you could too. What are you doing?'

'Shepherding children. My two are in bed. I'm not sure about Lee.'

'What? Lee?'

'Since I visited Holly, we've been getting these phone calls. No sound at the other end, just someone breathing. I know it's him, I know he's trying to scare me.'

'I'll go and see him, then.'

'No, definitely not. You won't go and see him. Don't go anywhere near him, just listen. Why do you always try to fix things?'

'I'm listening. But in the end, we need to go see him again. Probably not what you wanted to hear.'

'I've been there twice.'

'If you're getting phone calls, tell the Department of Education. Or the police.'

'No. I'm in trouble already for going to his house.'

'What then?'

'I could phone Lisa Charles, see what she can do.'

'Who?'

'Police officer who dealt with Rose when she shoplifted.'

'If she can't do anything, I mean, if the police say their hands are tied, I'll go see him.'

'That won't help.'

'I won't go and see him as a psychologist, I'll go and see him as Julia's friend. That's all.'

'I don't want you to do that.'

'He's a coward. He abuses women and children behind closed doors. He won't pick on somebody his own size.'

'Don't be so sure.'

Kate was quiet on the other end of the line.

Julia regretted calling her. 'Don't get in trouble.'

'With Lee? Come on.'

'I just heard a car outside. I have to go.'

'I miss you, and I love you,' she said. 'Sleep well and –'

Julia set down the receiver and cut her off. Kate's voice stayed in the room with her, and the events of the night stayed too. She knew she wouldn't sleep well.

The following day, Julia watched Rose in class, sitting on the floor next to the basket, rocking back and forth and whispering to the eagle.

What did Rose think about the war between Julia and her stepfather? Did she know about the dead phone calls and where Lee went at night? Did Lee think about Julia as often as Julia thought about him?

Rose continued to murmur to the eagle and stroke her head. Once, she looked up and smiled.

Three o'clock arrived, and it was time to go home.

On Wednesday, Julia arrived home, patted Bonnie, and walked to the mailbox. In the box lay five letters. Four bills and one unmarked envelope with no name, address or stamp. Junk mail, thought Julia, some advertising blitz.

She ripped open the flap and pulled out the single card, but couldn't understand what she saw. It was a photograph, a poorly focused one. Why would someone send a blurred photograph of a house? Julia studied it, confused and shaking her head, she tipped it into the sunlight. She whispered, 'My house.' Julia squinted in the harsh light and bent her head to throw a shadow over the photograph and study it. 'What is this about? Why would someone send me a picture of my own house?'

She pulled it closer and peered hard at characters in the poorly focused shot. Julia felt her eyes widen and loom over the bottom left-hand corner where Bonnie ran over the grass. The photograph shook in her hand. In the corner of the photograph, Bonnie ran at play with Ben and Claire.

22

Kate's Threats

She dragged herself up Black Mountain.

Kate said, 'I'm going to see Lee.'

'No. Just wait. The police don't see how they can trace a photograph. And when they spoke to Lee, he emphatically denied it. And he denied calling my house.'

'Of course he did. Come on.' She crossed her wrists. '"Why yes, officers, it happened just like Julia said it did. Please take me away. Not too tight."'

'That, darling, won't help.'

'You won't let me help.'

'The police say they're powerless unless they catch him doing it. What can you do that the police can't?'

'Let's just say I have an understanding of men like Lee. I've studied their psychology. Lee's a mutant, he's cruel, an oppressor. He needs to taste oppression.'

They hiked in silence with a cool wind at their backs and Julia said, 'He said something strange: "Your friend Dr Selby knows more than she lets on."'

'I know his taste for vengeance. He can't see a way out, without losing face.'

'He's dangerous.'

'Sure he's dangerous. To women and children, but not to grown men, or to me. He's a coward.'

'How do you know that?'

'Read *Notes From Underground*.'

'What? What does that have to do with Lee?'

'The hero is standing next to a table in a pub. Accidentally, he blocks the path of an army officer who, with no warning or explanation, grabs him by the shoulders and moves him to another place. The officer walks past him, like he can't see him. The hero can't forget the humiliation, he's filled with rage. He follows the officer home to learn his name and plan an act of vengeance. He borrows a fine coat with a raccoon collar, and goes to the Nevsky Prospect hunting for him. With the officer coming straight towards him, three paces away, the hero holds his course and crashes into the officer, crashes into his shoulder. The officer walks on, doesn't even look around. Victory. Vindication.'

'Victory?'

'Yes.'

'That's silly.'

'Yes.'

'A story about payback that nobody sees.'

'A story about Lee.'

They stood on the hillside over the purring city; boats on the lake etched on glass. Kate and Julia didn't look at each other.

Kate said, 'For Lee, payback is the natural condition, the point of living.'

'What?'

Kate looked over. 'This city doesn't understand Lee because it doesn't understand the hostility just under the skin in men. She's the mother who swears her son isn't the serial rapist terrifying the neighbourhood. She's always the last to know.'

'You're not making any sense today.'

'Maybe.'

They walked quietly down the mountain.

Julia dreamed with her soul close to her body. By 3 a.m., she began to toss and grind her teeth, then heard the knock on the door. Slipping out of bed, she threw on a robe and saw the woman standing on the porch in a trench coat knotted at the waist.

'Ms Honeychurch?'

'You're back.'

'Ms Honeychurch, I'm – '

'What do you want at this hour?'

Stark leggy trees stood behind her in moonlight.

The woman looked up and down the street. 'There's a cheerful snobbery in this neighbourhood. More than a few Saabs.'

'I said, what do you want?'

'Ms Honeychurch...'

'Be quick.'

'We've been watching you.'

'Again? No point in throwing on this robe. You've seen it all.'

'The last time, of course, I came about your failures at work. So you know why I'm here tonight.'

'No.'

'It's obvious, Ms Honeychurch.'

'What are you talking about?'

'Love, Ms Honeychurch. Love and work are all we have. It was clear from the first day we started watching you that you botched both of them. I mean, really? If we could see it so clearly, why couldn't you?'

'See what?'

'You're a balls-up. A failure. I mean, very grand, all this, thinking, "I might have been a failure at work, and with my family, but once I delivered a child from an evil man." Called self-delusion.'

Julia looked away.

'Anyway, Ms Honeychurch, to get to the point, I've come to inform you that we've known for some time now that you've been a fool. This woman, Kate, isn't what she seems. She's mannish, a little vain, childless and very sorry. With Brian, you got a dull one, that's for sure. But with Kate, you got trouble.'

'No.'

'Oh please, Ms Honeychurch, smarten up.'

'That's a lie.'

'A lie? Which part? Ms Honeychurch, you've thrown yourself into this delusion with colossal vitality. We're impressed. But this isn't a grainy old black and white movie.'

'You don't understand. She's sensitive.'

'Sensitive? Sensitive to what?'

'Kate's self-assured, eloquent, a teacher, the basis for all my hope.'

'Oh?'

'When she came to Wattle Street, she would circle a problem, drive into its heart. It was glorious to watch.'

'Drive into what, Ms Honeychurch?'

'You mock me.'

'Kate may be glorious to watch, but you get her troubles as a side benefit. And they don't come for free.'

'That's not fair.'

'Ruth has been uncannily correct, about everything, Ms Honeychurch. Kate, the expert, is starting to misfire, miscalculate.'

'But –'

'You and Ruth are teachers, Ms Honeychurch. Kate left teaching long ago.'

'No –'

'Ms Honeychurch– and please listen carefully – scandal holds far greater danger than physical harm. Understand me? Far greater danger.'

'I'm not frightened of scandal.'

'Then you should be. Take my advice. Chain yourself to your family. Padlock yourself to a post in the yard and throw away the key. Let your love for Kate blow quietly away.'

'I can't do that.'

'Quietly away, Ms Honeychurch.'

'No.'

'More failure, Ms Honeychurch.'

Julia shook her head. 'No.'

'Please. Think about it.'

'Is that all?'

'For now.'

'Well, thank you for coming.'

'I can't say "my pleasure", Ms Honeychurch, because these visits are never enjoyable. I'd rather pull teeth. But somebody has to do it, and we do get to see Canberra.'

'Good for you. Watch the tricycle in the drive.'

'Thank you, I will.' And she disappeared into the night.

23

Lisa Charles at School

In a soft pearly rain, Julia folded her umbrella and stepped into the school. Lisa Charles arrived in uniform, and Julia motioned her to the childless classroom. In a circle of low-backed chairs, Lisa sat with the upright paramilitary bearing of an officer. Principal Bob Richmond spread over both sides of his student chair and Jeremy, pale and earnest, parted his lips in an abortive attempt to smile. After Ruth made a nervous circuit of the unit, she came back into the circle of chairs to hear what the police had to say about Lee.

As was her custom, Lisa barely said hello before she came straight to the point. 'We can't do anything about the phone calls, not at the moment anyway. If they were longer, and more frequent, we could trace them. The recording from your answering machine is just heavy breathing.'

'That's what he does.'

'We have no way of knowing if the heavy breathing is Lee or someone else. Have there been any more?'

'Two last night. I still think he's watching my house.'

'When I visited Lee's house yesterday,' said Lisa, 'he swore up and down that he hadn't seen or spoken to you since he found you with Holly. He said that you've been harassing his family for some weeks now, that you turn up unannounced and make trouble. He said you were abusive towards Holly.'

'That's a lie,' said Julia.

'I need to tell you that Holly said very little, she sat huddled on that sofa in that strange blue and brown sitting room. But when Lee asked for support, when he asked Holly to back up his claims, she...'

'What claims?'

'That you were causing trouble to his family.'

Julia shook her head.

'She agreed. Rose did too.'

'Rose said that?'

'I'm afraid so. Holly didn't look up, you know how she keeps her eyes to the floor, but she did support Lee's story.'

Julia raised her finger, and fumbled her words. 'So now, he...' she put her hand over her mouth. 'You're saying it's my word against Lee's, and my word against Holly's. You believe them.'

'Julia, please listen. At no point this morning have I taken sides. Is that clear? I'm reporting Lee's response to your complaint, and Lee's complaint about you. He told me he might lodge a complaint with the minister of education, and Holly would back him on that complaint.'

The feeling of injury grew and Julia started to shake. Her face had a scarlet burn, and she tried not to sit there and plan spiteful revenge against Lee. Kate had been right about him. The room and Lisa Charles drifted out of focus for a time.

'Julia?' said Bob.

They waited and watched her wet eyes and quivering mouth until she could speak.

'They're lying. They're both lying!'

Bob hadn't seen her cry before. Head down in her own classroom, surrounded by her work and rules, her face smeared with tears. Lisa reached over in a gesture of comfort, then pulled back as Julia brushed her hand away.

'This has gone on for weeks. He threatened me, he threatened my family with that photograph. He makes those phone calls. My phone number is unlisted. How did he get it? He wants to scare us, and he has scared us. But I'm not going to back down.'

'Julia, he gave us his camera,' said Lisa, 'the little Kodak, the only camera they have.'

Julia stared. 'Or so he says.'

Ruth bristled. 'Exactly. I mean, really, the only camera he's got! Surely you people won't fall for such an obvious trick.'

Lisa ignored her. 'We'll have forensics test it against the photograph you gave us. Cameras, especially their lenses, have aberrations, individual characteristics like fingerprints. Lee probably knows that, but he wasn't worried, he just handed over the camera.'

To Julia, it was obvious how this would play out. 'Then it's a different camera.'

'I have to say that I tried to read him,' said Lisa. 'I watched his body language and listened to his tone of voice when he answered my questions. He seemed to flare when I asked about the phone calls. He didn't stay cool, didn't look away. I'm not certain if that means he did or didn't made those phone calls or send the photographs, but he certainly didn't like being blamed for them.'

'You're not sure, but I am. He takes the moral high ground over this terrible injustice to his family. I've seen it. What bullshit.'

'That may be,' said Lisa, 'and you know we'll try to support you. But, for now, I have to advise you to stay away from the Cavanaugh house. There's nothing we can do at the moment, and nothing you can do either. Stay away.'

Bob nodded with each word that he thought was important, 'That's right, that's right. The department can't support you on this thing if, ah, if this Lee fellow makes a complaint. After all, he's warned us. No way the department can support you.'

'Can't support me, or won't?'

'Stay away from his house,' said Bob, 'and it's best if you're not alone with Rose. Make certain that Jeremy or Ruth are in the room with you when you talk to Rose.'

'I'm her teacher.'

'That's right. You're her teacher. Just do your job as a teacher,' said Bob. 'Leave the social work to the social workers.'

Julia shook her head slowly.

'I'll do what I can,' said Lisa in a slow, warm voice. 'The police want him as badly as you do. But we need to catch him without him catching us, especially without him catching you. It's difficult to determine what he knows about the law, but he's smarter than he looks. All this home-boy stuff, backward and country, is an act he puts on. Experienced law-breakers know the law. And technically, Rose Cavanaugh is Lee's child. That gives him leverage and privileges over Rose that you don't have.'

They sat and looked at her. Julia was broken and subdued, thinking, 'They don't believe me.' She wanted to scream in their faces but she carried the leaden curse that she'd always carried – she could see their point of view. No matter how disloyal Rose and Holly and Bob had been, how loaded with betrayal and hypocrisy towards Rose, or towards her, she could always see their point of view. Full of interior rules that checked her from standing up and shouting in Bob's face, leaving spittle on his cheek.

She leaned back in her chair and nodded. 'I understand. I'll stay away.'

24

Kate Visits Lee

At first, Julia didn't tell Kate about the humiliation she suffered in the meeting. On the dark east face of Aranda bushland, in cooling shade, Julia sat on a log and cried with her head down on her knees.

Kate whispered that she loved her, promised to stand by her and asked her to talk. 'Please tell me. Please tell me what's caused this. Is it me?'

Julia shook her head and didn't speak.

Kate asked again, 'Please tell me,' then waited on the log in the forest.

Julia didn't talk. She wept quietly with her face down.

After ten minutes of wordless crying, Kate understood. Her face turned as white as cotton, then it turned deep red. She kept her warm hand on Julia's shoulder as turmoil boiled in her head and her fingers began to tighten. She waited until Julia stopped shuddering. A slight breeze in the forest and both of them quiet.

Then Kate said in a calm voice, 'Let's go.'

'It's nearly dark,' said Julia. 'I have to go home.'

Bats flitted over the tree canopy.

'Just come with me.'

'What for?'

'Please do this for me. It won't take long.'

Julia followed her.

She rolled her Volvo, heavy and solid, down the road under Giralang street lights.

Julia said, 'We can't. You know I can't go there.'

Kate pulled up against the curb at a playground over the road from Lee's house, reached across Julia and opened her door, 'I'll pick you up in five minutes.'

'No. Don't do this.'

'Get out.'

Julia stood on the kerb feeling exposed.

Kate circled and Julia watched her drive down the street and coast into Lee's driveway. Julia slid into shadow under a she-oak. Kate stepped out and walked over the lawn with the same toys and tussocks and bare patches underfoot. A dim glow from the lounge room lit her way to the glass front door. The porch light was off. Two knocks. No response. Three more. A minute passed with no reply and Julia prayed he wouldn't come to the door. She watched as the porch light snapped on and Holly's face appeared.

'Hi, Holly.'

She was startled. 'Oh, um, you…' Silence.

'Is Lee here?'

'Um-yeah. He's here.' She called in a muted voice back into the house, 'Lee.'

He walked out of the brown gloom. Even to Julia over the road he looked uneasy. 'What do you want?'

'Hi, Lee. Listen. I just need some advice about my radiator. Trying to get home and it's heating up. I remembered you lived close by. Mind giving me some help?'

Lee was suspicious. For a moment, he studied Kate's eyes, level with his. She wore jeans and a sweat shirt; he would know she hadn't come from work. Julia, watching from the park, beseeching him to go back into his house and shut the door.

'Radiator?' he said.

'I think so. I'll open the bonnet, if you can have a look.'

'I'll get my shoes. Hang about.'

Julia watched. Lee must know what she wanted, he couldn't be that stupid. Maybe he knew and didn't want to look frightened in front of Holly and Rose.

He moved back into the gloom and returned to the doorway in thongs. Looking straight into Kate's face, he smiled, 'Let's have a squiz.'

They walked to Kate's Volvo in the dim light cast from the porch light that diminished as they neared the car. Kate leaned into the driver's side and opened the bonnet. The two of them peered under.

'Okay, where's the problem?' asked Lee.

'We're going to talk about Julia.'

Lee moved out from under the bonnet and stepped back. 'Julia? Haven't seen Julia for a while. What's your problem?'

Kate seemed to grow before the enemy, she looked down on him. 'You're quick to tell me you haven't seen her, Lee. We both know you have.'

'What?' Fine sweat beaded on his hollow face. 'What are we talking about here?'

'You look scared.'

'I'm not scared of anything,' Lee's boast was shrill and catlike.

She moved closer to Lee's face and Julia knew Kate smelled beer and cigarettes on his breath, and sweat. 'Let's drop the polite conversation.' She moved closer and again Lee stepped back. 'I know you've had your hands on Rose, and I'll see you hang for it.'

A flash of white came off Lee's eyes. 'Fuck you.'

'You're trying to scare Julia. I want to be perfectly clear: you'd better pray the cops get to you before I do.'

The moon sailed free of a cloud bank and Julia could see their faces reflecting white.

Lee pointed at Kate, speared his finger through the air. 'You fucking dyke. *Leave.*'

Kate pulled her hand out of her pocket, raised it, and leaned poking into his chest, stabbed his clavicle. 'The cops will give you a fair trial. Not me.'

'What?'

'Got it?'

Lee backed up a step as Kate stabbed with her finger, as if trying to bruise him. 'Fuck off,' Lee complained.

'Stop me.'

He stepped back again, and Kate stepped forward. Julia saw her shadow dart over the ground.

'Now that I have your full attention... Do I have your full attention, Lee?'

'Leave, you cunt.'

'If you do anything to try to scare Julia, anything, send any more photographs, I'll follow you. Know what I'll do when I catch you?' Kate poking her finger hard into his chest. 'I said, do you know what I'm going to do to you when I catch you alone?'

'Fuck off, cunt.'

'Quick surgery with a knife. One snip. Your troubles being bent are over. Freed from this life of misery.'

Kate serving up spoonfuls of hate, Lee standing firm, a smear of sweat on his forehead gleaming in the cold night. She leaned into him. 'I should have done this weeks ago.'

Lee seemed to look around for a weapon, a tyre iron, a rock. He picked up the metal tricycle, held it over his head, cocked in one hand and leaned towards her, 'Fuck off. *Now.*'

Kate stood with her hands open. 'Do it.'

'You cunt.'

She smiled and stepped forward, arms wide. Lee raised the metal to crash down into her face. Kate smiled and she raised her finger to poke him again, stepped forward as Lee stepped back with his arm cocked, ready to break her head. She knew she had him.

Holding the tricycle over his head, Lee stared at her, then dumped the tricycle on the grass. "I know what you're trying to do.' He walked over the lawn through broken toys, jumped the steps and banged on the glass front door. '*Open the fucking door.* I'm calling the cops.'

Kate stood in the middle of the lawn, one hand deep in her pocket, the other hand dangling with a finger pointing down. Curtains pulled to one side tipped a column of yellow light onto the lawn. Holly looked out.

Lee stood facing the door, '*Let me in.*'

Julia in the park moved out from under the tree.

Kate walked to her Volvo and slammed down the bonnet, climbed in, and backed out of the driveway. Julia waited and hoped she would drive past but she didn't.

She stopped along the kerb, leaned across and opened the passenger door. 'Get in.'

Julia bent over and crawled into the Volvo, lay down out of sight, and said, 'You idiot. Do you realise what you've done?'

Kate said nothing as they drove towards her empty flat in Aranda, the Volvo lurching around corners. The index finger on her right hand was obviously hurt, maybe broken. She lifted it up off the steering wheel, pointing at the moon, and she seemed happy.

25

Giving Shelter

'And am no more worthy to be called thy son:
make me as one of thy hired servants.'

The morning breeze carried the sound of children. Julia watched from her classroom. Beneath her pale window, Jeremy smiled at Rose, a white-hearted child, spread his hands out to instruct her. Rose watched the eagle and listened.

Jeremy once told her that he stayed away from others in the city who cared for orphaned and injured animals. They fought each other, he said, over who cared the most, or who cared better; they fought like wolves. The intoxication of doing good deeds gave them self-righteous power to use against their enemies, and their enemies were other caregivers. They faced each other in court and took hostages in their cause.

Jeremy helped Rose lift a piece of meat from the saucer and Julia wondered if a band of brothers would have embraced Jeremy ten thousand years ago, if his kindness and gentleness would have bought him a place in the tribal order or carried denunciation, slowed him like a withered leg and dragged him to an early grave. Jeremy would have fed his nieces and nephews and covered them in the morning rain as the other men left for the day. But maybe they would expect more and he would refuse and they would cast him out. Lee would have survived ten thousand years ago because Lee was born with no kindness in him, hunting through forests and killing with a smile, raping other men's daughters. Or maybe not. Maybe Lee was born with kindness smothered by grudges against the world, or the city that harboured him, and the family that left him tricked and disgraced. Or so he believed.

Rose touched the eagle's beak and the eagle took a small piece. She sat back against the tree and smiled and Jeremy smiled with her.

They walked among trees on the oval. Leaves blew about them showing their silvery undersides and Julia held Kate's hand up, pulled it closer to see the splint around her index finger.

'Does it hurt?'

'Yes. It didn't hurt much at the time.'

'I've been waiting for a visit from the police,' said Julia.

'Not likely.'

'What possessed you to go there?'

'I wanted to.'

'Now he wants both of us. I've never seen anyone so angry.'

'No. Lee wasn't angry. He was scared.'

'I don't think so.'

'He's scared, and he's bitter.'

'You threatened him. And you hit him.'

'No. You're wrong. I didn't hit him. I poked him to get his full attention. He seemed to have trouble listening, so I poked him. Nothing more.'

Julia shook her head. 'He'll tell the police, or the department.'

'I don't think so. He won't tell them about me. A man who runs away from women doesn't fit his tough-boy likeness in the glass.'

Julia was surprised at Kate's certainty. She talked as if she had the upper hand.

'Nobody will believe him, and he knows that. He'll never admit that he backed down from me. He knows he'd have to make up a story about protecting Holly or defending Rose, and the story would fall flat, never ring true. His stories don't chime, they don't win him friends. He's no good at fabricating good lies, he lacks imagination. He lacks practice and skill at sounding credible.'

'He made up a credible story about me. Remember? I'm the one pestering Holly.'

Kate turned and watched a car rush by. As it disappeared, she stepped forward on the grass and said, 'He knows I'll go back and visit him if he goes anywhere near you. It's done now, and it felt good at the time.'

Their shoulders touched as they walked quietly over clipped grass, with the bandaged finger swinging at Kate's side. Julia didn't know where she was leading them, and didn't care.

'I wander, at night you know, through woodlands and down bicycle paths.'

'You told me.'

'Last night, about midnight on the path from Aranda up past the Grove to the Bindubi underpass, the cold air washed over my face and I started to feel better. My finger was throbbing. Up ahead, I could see this figure. I'd been walking so fast trying to burn off my anger that I overtook her before I knew it. A woman out there at midnight. I'm not sure why the woman would be alone in the middle of the night, strolling along thinking about family or the boyfriend or great literature, and suddenly this shadow looms up behind her in the dark, big as a man. I didn't mean to frighten her, I tried to slow down but I frightened her badly anyway. She started to run, and I called out but she kept running and I watched her disappear. I felt sick. Poor woman thought I was going to jump her.'

'It's the way things are. She has to fear you.'

'Demonised by someone I'd never met.'

'You can understand why she ran.'

'Of course I can. I scare people. I didn't take it personally. It was shameful, that's all, that I terrified her. I wandered most of last night thinking about it, thinking about who she was, and how she must have felt. Wishing I could talk to her.'

She paused for a moment, withdrawn into some vision, then said, 'You know, we don't know Rose at all, do we? You've spent all this time with her, visited her family, and you teach her every day and plan her life, and you don't really know her, what she hopes, or believes, or dreams about.'

'No, I don't.'

Kate said nothing for a time, then mumbled, 'Elvis has left the auditorium.'

'What?'

'Elvis has left the auditorium.'

'What does that mean?'

'Part of the reason I've been walking lately is I need time to think. I've had these spells.'

'Spells?

'I'll be standing in front of a group of two hundred students, talking and talking, then talking some more. Lord knows I do nothing but talk all day. My head goes into automatic, and the sermon carries on without me. My mouth is in autopilot. I can float to the ceiling and watch the performance.'

'You're bored with it.'

'I'm bored with the sound of my own voice. I'm not needed down there any more, so my body floats around the room and watches this woman spraying the crowd with pretty words. I'm disgusted with myself, and I can't stop thinking about Lee. So I quit my own head, leave the podium for a time and hover near the ceiling, look down on this woman lecturing. I watch the whole piece of theatre from above. Omniscience.'

Julia didn't know how to respond.

'But in the middle of a lecture last week, I stopped. While I was gone, the words stopped and the sermon stopped. The students looked at each other, started to giggle and whisper. Some of them looked at their watches. I'm not sure why that's so demeaning, to look up and see them angling their wrist in dim light to read the time. It means nothing.'

'Your reviews are good. Students trust you.'

'I had to return to the podium in a hurry because it all started to go pear-shaped. I rushed back and tried to bluff my way through and take up where I'd left off. It was nearly impossible.'

'Have you talked to anyone about this?'

'No. This defenceless, pathetic fraud stood before them, and there wasn't a shred of pity for her.'

Julia walked quietly at her side.

Kate suddenly stopped. 'Why do you stay with Brian?'

Julia shook her head, trying to understand the abrupt change in subject. 'We've been through all this.'

'Let's go through it again.'

'You have to understand how young I was. I didn't know that people could feel like we do now. How could I? He's so boring that I want to scream. I want to fly, he wants to work on his car. But he's not sentimental, and he's not cruel.'

Kate reached over and held Julia's hand. A cold breeze swept down the street clattering leaves in ribbon gums along the curb. Julia wished she'd brought a jumper.

'In a good marriage,' she said, 'you figure out how to live with someone without bothering them. I knew a woman who moved around the corner from her husband into a different house. The marriage worked out so well they stayed that way, a stunning success. He rushes over to visit her three times a day.'

'As one does.'

'Well, as I would if we could. We manage three times a week.'

They were quiet, and Julia said, 'What about your parents?'

'What about them?'

'Their marriage. You never talk about them.'

Kate sighed. 'Mother is quiet, seems to harbour some injury she never talked about, and I was brought up by a deaf mute.'

'A deaf mute?'

'Functionally. He was a competent mechanic, not the best, and with no genius for wealth. He lost his own business early on, and after that he worked for somebody else. Good with his hands, but he never said much. He would take me into his old wooden garage, his kingdom with carpet over the dirt floor under his car, and teach me how to fix motors and lawnmowers. I would drift off and sit in the corner with *Bleak House* or *Huckleberry Finn* on my lap and disappoint him, not because he wanted me to become a mechanic. He didn't. But he tried to find something in common with me. He wanted me to do things with him, but I didn't want to do things with my father, and that hurt him. Work had scoured all the fun out of him, thinking about all the useless things he'd made with his hands, a body worn out from hoping. He was trapped.'

They walked into softening darkness. Julia knew Kate was thinking about ineptitude and sanity and regretting the way she'd spent her days, listing sins of omission. And about Rose sleeping sweetly with moonlight on her face, butter-coloured hair on the pillow as Lee bricked up her bedroom window as punishment.

26

Jamison

'Let them live, but let them be hewers of wood and drawers of water unto all the congregation, as the princes had promised.'

There'd been no dead phone calls for two nights. Julia drove to Jamison for milk and a treat for Claire and Ben, said she'd be back in ten minutes. Brian sat on the lounge, his face lit by the flashing TV.

She eased her front bumper close to the brick wall in the parking lot and sat for a moment listening to the tick of the cooling motor. She looked through the windscreen at the cold moonless night. Black Mountain tower was shrouded in heavy clouds and the sky was the colour of dark slate. She wanted to finish and drive home. Wind gusted over the road and light drizzle hit the windscreen. The massed tree branches made a fabric against the rain and a row of blinking yellow lights on the roof of the Jamison Inn filled the car with a vague uneasiness. The parking lot was almost empty.

Julia stepped onto the bitumen, turned, locked the door and walked from deep shadow into the lit Jamison Centre.

After paying the cashier, she walked back to the Mazda, opened the door and sat ready to swing her legs in. A hand reached out and gripped her hair, pushed her face into her lap. Bent double, Julia tried to suck in air. She couldn't see who dug their fingers into her scalp. She struggled, kicked out and twisted her head around to wrench free. The man spread dirty brown boots on the pavement and leaned down on her, kept her doubled up and pushed the air out of her lungs. Julia reached up and grabbed two of his fingers, bent them sideways off her head.

'Bitch,' he muttered, and pulled her hand away.

She knew she would die there. Full of adrenalin, she flung one leg into the car and tried to slam the door against his hand. He jerked the door open and a bolt of pain shot to her shoulder.

'Move over,' he said.

Julia sat fast in the driver's seat with her hands on the wheel.

He tried to pull her out. 'Move over,' a low growl in the back of his throat, 'or I'll cut you.' The yobbo accent had disappeared; he was suddenly educated.

She slowly lifted her legs over the gearstick and slid into the passenger side. He dropped into the driver's seat and shut the door, laid his arm across her chest and locked the passenger side door. He smelled like faeces and mouldy dirt from under a house, and he'd imprisoned her.

'What do you want?' she said.

'We know a fair bit about you.' The drizzle had plastered his scant hair to his skull.

Julia looked out through the windscreen and tucked her hands between her knees to hide the shaking. She held her keys there.

'We know you visit Kate in Aranda,' he said in a high scattered voice. 'Does your husband know how often you lick that dyke?'

Julia was focused on the smell of cigarettes, sweat and broken drains coming off him, trying to decide if she'd vomit.

'What do you want?'

'Just a yarn.' He tried to be country, but it was forced. He reached down to his ankle, pulled out a long, black-handled knife, and tapped the blade on the steering wheel. Tap. Tap. Tap.

She turned to unlock the passenger side door, thinking, 'Where are the people'?

Lee grabbed her wrist and banged it against the dash. She closed her eyes in pain.

He held the knife under her chin. 'Give me your keys. Now. *Right now*.'

'No.'

With a deft move, he stabbed down between her legs. She'd lost sight of the knife and thought he'd cut her, bent over ready for the pain. He grabbed the keys, rolled down the window, and tossed them clattering onto the bitumen. Then he reached to the floor, felt around for the knife, and started tapping it again on the steering wheel. Tap. Tap. Tap.

'Get out,' she yelled. 'My husband expects me home. He knows where I am.'

'I'll go in a minute.' Tapping the knife on the steering wheel. 'You sent your girlfriend to see me.'

'That's not true.'

'And you sat in the park and watched.'

The cold tickle of the knife against Julia's ear.

'You don't understand.' A new helplessness pressed down on her. There was no way to explain to Lee what had happened because no words she knew would convince him. 'It's not true. You have to believe me.'

'I don't believe you, and I don't want you or the girlfriend near my house. Ever. Do you understand?

'Yes.'

'You're trying to wreck my family, you and the dyke. You wreck my family, I wreck yours. Got it?'

She didn't answer.

'How much does Principal Bob know about you two?'

She sat quietly.

'How 'bout your kids? How much do they know?'

Julia turned and shouted in his face, '*Get out,*' leaning towards the knife, her chest thumping. '*Leave me alone.*'

'Just seems fair, doesn't it? You talk to my kids about my business, I talk to your kids about your business, what you get up to in the afternoons. What goes around comes around.'

'Get out.'

'I get out when I feel like it. If the girlfriend visits my family again, I visit yours.'

She sat.

'Got wax in your fuckin' ears? *Listen to me.*' Spittle on her. 'School-teachers are a bit slow, a bit simple, I get that. In short simple words, you wreck my family, I wreck yours.'

Julia stared through the windscreen, trying to look full of anger.

'Tell me,' he said. 'What makes you think you're fuckin' better than me? A fucking schoolteacher. A fucking teacher of all things, telling us how to live.' He spat pieces of hate in her face. 'See, the good thing about being a plumber is me and my mates find things out, what happens in this town. Better than anyone. We know a lot of secrets. And I'm not licking somebody's cunt like your girlfriend is. You phoney bitch. The department needs to know that. If she comes to my house again, I'll take the department to Dr Selby's house, personally.'

The blade flashed yellow off the blinking lights on the Jamison Inn. Julia looked through the windscreen at drizzle and rocking eucalypt branches. She gripped the seat under her thighs as Lee hissed in her ear.

She turned and looked into his face and said, 'When the police hear about this, I won't be able to save your family.'

He tried to look menacing, condescending, he smiled and slipped into a nasal drawl. 'Fine, I'll shoot the bitch.'

'I know you've been calling my house – '.

'Fine, I said. I'll shoot her dead. You have my word on that. I promise I'll shoot her if she comes near my house again. Fact is, I might shoot her anyway.'

'You sent those pictures. The police know it.'

He glowered, twisted with hatred, 'You set me up.'

'Always somebody else.'

A security guard walked to the glass entrance of the centre, stepped outside, and looked over the parking lot.

Lee stared at him, looked back at Julia and said with a half-smile, 'He won't come out here. Too dark.'

They watched the guard turn back through the sliding glass doors.

'No luck tonight, eh, teacher?' he grinned through yellow teeth.

'What do you want?'

'I told you.'

She sat with her hands under her legs.

'Listen, cunt. You've been warned,' eyes cold with hate.

Julia started to shake.

Lee noticed, and he smiled. He waited, watching her hands and the side of her face, using up the time. 'See ya,then.'

He slid the knife into its ankle sheath, opened the driver's side door and stepped to the front of the car. He stood facing her and opened his fly, urinated on the bitumen, splashing and making a puddle, then turned, zipped his trousers and loped off.

27

Orphan

'Then came Peter to him, and said, Lord, how oft shall my
brother sin against me, and I forgive him? Till seven times?'

Julia missed a week of school. Pictures of Lee bothered her sleep but
she didn't telephone the police. She dreamt about lighted windows
in the school and red chatter flowing through open doorways, the
blue promise of a clear day unfolding through trees in the street. Over
breakfast, she decided to go to work as normal, but she couldn't eat.

On the way to Wattle Street, malevolence crackled in the air and
Julia knew Rose wouldn't come to school, that Lee would keep her
locked up. And the nestling eagle had shaken off her illness and Jeremy
said he couldn't wait for Rose. He needed to place the eagle in a nest
soon, even if Rose couldn't come. He would place her in the pinnacle
of a giant she-oak on the river, check her well-being each day and make
sure that she and her nest-mates fared well.

'If we don't move quickly,' he said, 'and foster her in the next few
days, she'll live a long life, maybe fifty years in Taronga Zoo.' It was a
matter of timing, and he painted images in words soaked in colour and
tragedy, and more failure. The images drove them.

The eagle still feared people, and that was part of Jeremy's plan. She
flattened in her box when other people came into view, rocked back
onto her tail and slashed at them with her talons if they moved too
close. For everyone, except Rose and Jeremy, she maintained a healthy
state of mistrust. She was two-thirds brown feathers flecked in sunlight
with some gold, and one-third snowy white down. With her new long
brown tail feathers and wing feathers, she looked more like an eagle.

Rose arrived late in the morning and sat down by the basket. She didn't talk.

Jeremy and Julia decided to move as planned. Jeremy carried the eagle in a box out to the car and they drove to Lyneham. The vet, John Glue, asked Jeremy to lift her from the box and hold her down on a stainless steel table. She struggled against Jeremy, her talons rang against the metal table.

Julia felt sick from the smell of disinfectant and cat urine, and the mournful barking of dogs.

Rose watched.

John Glue said, 'We don't need to bother with a general anaesthetic. Birds don't feel much pain.'

'Why is she protesting then?' said Julia.

'Hates being held down, restrained, the indignity of it all. Now Rose, you'd squeal too if I pinned you down on this cold table.' He chuckled and winked at Rose, but Rose frowned and looked down.

John took pliers from the drawer, parted the fluffy down at the base of the eagle's wing, and found the pin. He braced his left hand against her body, manoeuvred around Jeremy, who pressed the eagle down on the table. 'You okay?'

Jeremy nodded.

John gripped the end of the pin with pliers and pulled with his face set hard. The pin didn't come.

Rose squinted and winced with her hands stiff at her sides.

John tugged at the pin, the eagle chittered, he pulled again and the eagle chittered again. With a jerk, he pulled and the pin gave way. He showed it to Rose, a long stainless steel rod. He examined the spot where the pin came out, felt along the humerus. 'It's fine,' he said. 'Rock her for us, Jeremy.'

Jeremy held the eagle up by the middle of her body with her head pointing towards the vet, rocking her from side to side on an axis from her beak through her body to her tail. The left wing, then the right wing drooped as he rolled her.

'She'll have no trouble,' said John. 'Symmetrically perfect.'

Jeremy lowered her back into the box.

Ranger Mel Davidson drove his Toyota, with Jeremy in front. Rose and Julia sat in the back with the eagle in a box between them. When Jeremy introduced Mel to Rose, he smiled and tried to shake her hand but she pulled her hands into her lap, sat back and eyed the gang-gangs on Mel's sleeve.

Jeremy turned to Rose. 'If we hold off much longer, she might leap out of the nest when Mel leaves her there. She could spiral into the Murrumbidgee and float away. All our work for nothing.'

Julia thought of the eagle's wings spread in the water, spinning in green swirls and drifting around a bend in the river and out of sight.

They bounced along the dirt road with dust boiling out from under the Toyota.

Julia tried to clean up the wreckage from last week, get Lee out of her head. She would decide whether to tell Kate, but not today. They drove through silent stretches of high grass and she thought about Lee's knife more than once and thought about Kate all morning.

Rose leaned against Julia and murmured, 'Regal's dead.'

Julia sat for a moment and absorbed the news. She leaned close and kept her voice low. 'I'm sorry. Who would do such a thing?'

'They did it again. He came good, but they did it again, and he died.'

Julia knew that Rose felt the brunt of Lee's feelings of betrayal, his malicious brand of grieving. Rose would feel his fists or his belt, boozy spittle on her face. 'Is he trying to blame you?'

'Sort of. But he thinks it might be rangers.' She looked at the patch on Mel's sleeve, and Mel heard some of it, turned his head and listened as they bounced along over potholes.

'We'll talk about this later,' said Julia.

They parked and climbed out. A herd of cattle lowed from a hillside to the west, and magpies carolled from a dead tree. Sacred ibis with scimitar beaks careened over them on hushed wings and Rose watched them.

Jeremy hiked alongside Mel. He stumbled and seemed to lumber under the weight of the box. Mel carried the rope and carabineers for climbing, and Rose and Julia followed and took turns with the heavy bag of food for the eagle.

Jeremy asked Mel if he'd shot any pigs lately, which he had, but he didn't want to talk about it with Rose standing nearby. They turned to problems of the eagle's release.

'This pair already has two,' said Jeremy. 'Wonder if the adults will be stretched for food now.'

Rose walked through long grass, following the two men up hill. She watched a flock of jade-coloured parrots burst chattering overhead and she turned to Julia, 'Will we take her back if they don't feed her?'

'They'll feed her. But they may not catch enough food for all three.'

They stood on a cliff looking down on the river. The nest was cradled in a massive she-oak just inside the ACT border. The tree stood on the bank with water licking at its feet. In its crown sat the neat bundle of sticks, like a wash basket the size of a small car. They could see two white chicks, turkey-sized mounds of snow resting on a flat bed of green leaves.

'Try the binoculars,' said Mel, and handed his to Julia.

The chicks lay flat in the nest swaying gently in the top of the she-oak, as if they believed they were invisible.

'Have a look, Rose.' Julia handed the binoculars to her, she twisted them inward to fit her small face.

She squinted and studied them. 'They're beautiful,' she said.

Jeremy said, 'She's three or four weeks older than those two.'

'Will that matter?' said Julia.

'Shouldn't,' said Jeremy.

From the top of the escarpment, they stepped down between rocks and bushes, skating on slippery grass, their feet kicking stones out from under them. They reached out and caught bushes on the way down. Standing on the riverbank, they heard water lapping the river shore and saw pieces of log drifting by. Two adult eagles circled over the nest on open black wings in cerulean sky.

'See them, Rose?' said Mel.

She squinted in raw sunlight, and nodded.

At the bottom of the tree, Mel uncoiled a rope, tied it to a rock and tossed the rock fifteen metres up over the first limb, or tried to. He missed each time. 'Damn this thing,' he said, and he tried again. He tried four more times. 'You give it a try, Jeremy.'

Jeremy tied a carabineer to the rope, swung and tossed it up, but the carabineer banged against the trunk and bounced back at them. He tried again, and it bounced back again. He gathered the rope and looped it carefully on the ground, looked up at the limb, down at the looped rope, up again at the limb and tossed the carabineer. It sailed over the limb.

Mel turned to Jeremy. 'You bring the rabbits?'

'Julia's got them.'

Julia stood by Rose and wondered how much normal male chatter she had been exposed to.

Jeremy said, 'Rose, we need some muscle.'

Mel grabbed one end of the rope and tied it around his waist. They grabbed the other end and Mel half-shinnied up the trunk with Rose, Jeremy and Julia pulling on the rope; he was half-lifted up to the first limb fifteen metres above.

'Thanks,' he yelled down.

He free-climbed twenty metres working his way between limbs, hugging the trunk to shinny up long spaces between branches. A string tied to his belt snaked between limbs; it followed him up and marked his route.

Rose stood at the bottom of the she-oak with Jeremy, her head tipped back, honey-coloured hair whipping in the breeze, and a hand shading her eyes from the mounting sun.

After the long climb, Mel pulled himself over the lip of the nest and stood. 'Okay,' he shouted, 'put her in the bag.'

Jeremy opened the mouth of the bag and looked in at the three frozen rabbits. Julia tied the end of the string to a hole in the empty feed sack, and Jeremy peered into the box.

'Rose,' he said, 'do you want to say goodbye?'

She wagged her head no.

The eagle hunkered down in the box as if it didn't want to leave. Jeremy pinned her wings to her body and lifted. She hooked her beak into the newspaper and anchored herself with heavy talons.

Jeremy pulled her free and placed her head-first into the bag with the frozen rabbits. He looked up and yelled, 'Okay Mel.'

Mel stood on the nest and hauled the bag, just off the ground at first. It spun clockwise, then back. He strained at the weight on the string, pulled and the bag rose along the bark, through branches; it banged against the trunk of the tree. He pulled for two minutes and the two white eaglets at Mel's feet lay still as he pulled the dead weight over the lip of the nest.

The tree swayed in light wind. Mel crouched and reached into the bag, pulled the eagle onto the bed of green leaves next to the two others, then dropped the frozen rabbits beside her.

A hard gust from down river caused Mel to lose his balance. He dropped to his knees and grabbed a limb, crouched and held on. The crown whipped back and forth and he held on with both hands. The wind slashed at the nest and the three young eagles crouched.

The others watched him from the ground.

Julia's hand went over her mouth. She said, 'Oh no.'

Jeremy shouted, 'Come down.'

Mal stayed crouched on the nest with arms and a leg wrapped around the limb. After a minute, the wind settled and he yelled, 'Coming down.' Mal tied the empty bag to his belt, lowered himself over the lip of the nest and started down.

The two younger nestlings were starkly white on the green bed of leaves, they lay flat as the nest rocked in the wind and they eyed the new eagle.

Suddenly the new eagle stood up and spread her wings in the wind, flapping and gripping the nest with her talons. It startled the younger chicks.

Rose's eyes widened. 'She's going to fly.'

'Just practising,' said Jeremy. 'Hopefully she won't make an error and sail into the river.'

She had lain in a cardboard box for four weeks but caught the wind under her with purpose and skill.

Mel lowered himself hand over hand down the rope.

They packed the equipment in boxes and bags and followed Jeremy and Mel through long grass up the hill, all of them panting and warmed. They turned and looked down on the three eaglets on the nest. A hare burst from under Jeremy's feet, loped and bounded off like an antelope.

The parent eagles circled on high currents in blue sky, ignoring the hare and resting on the wind directly overhead, escorting them from the nest.

'How do you feel, Rose?' asked Jeremy.

Rose smiled.

'Thanks for coming.'

They sighted the four-wheel drive and beat towards it with a strong wind at their backs. The morning was temperate and full of some triumph, though Julia thought it might be premature.

Jeremy and Mel laughed and talked on the way home, forgot about Julia and Rose in the back seat and said they hoped the weather didn't break because a storm could blow the new eagle into the river.

Rose sat looking ahead with her hands in her lap; she had slipped into a blank stare; inaccessible.

Julia sat next to her thinking about pigs.

28

Marlene

Lying in bed that night, Julia travelled to the desert on a black horse under a red moon to visit Marlene in a corrugated-iron hut sheltering in sandhills north of Port Augusta. A howling dry wind sifted grit through windows and made skinny dogs huddle.

She thought about Rose, walking in long spring grass that morning, how Lee would stop her from walking close to Julia if he knew, maybe take a rifle and force her to lead him to the nest. 'Tomorrow,' she thought, 'I'll give Rose the same earring I shared with Marlene, and she'll keep it in her pocket and by her bed to help her choose between right and wrong. We'll be sisters, and she can wear it in her room and have my protection against Lee.'

The air that night smelled of rain. A deep westerly spilled a pink billow of clouds into blue sky. Streets in Cook would be glassy and black under smoky lamps. A moon soaked in wet light vanished as rain tapped on brittle gums in the yard. Their branches swishing against her window.

She thought about Kate before falling asleep. But she dreamed about the eagle, blasted from its nest by peppering rain, cart wheeling into the river on outstretched wings and floating away.

29

The Mare

The muttering thunder stopped at two in the morning, though rain swept over the house until four. The smell of dirt and wetness came in through Julia's window. In the dissolving night she lay awake, two or three stars left hanging in the open sky. The storm had been violent, and she knew the eagle had spun like a yellow box leaf into the chocolate river. She lay with this vision for an hour then slid out of bed and stepped onto the back veranda in warming sun. The yard was freshly washed. A slender mountain gum stood clean and white next to the fence, and candle barks were shining.

When Julia could bury her uneasiness no longer, she phoned Jeremy and left her family to meet him at Ginninderra Falls. Jeremy leaned against his car and had dark crescents under his eyes. They started up the slope to the crest of the hill where they could see over the swollen brown river and look into the nest. Jeremy always looked pensive, but the distracted silence on his face that morning made Julia's stomach knot. Jeremy was the expert, the one who dispelled their unfounded concerns, and he was afraid.

Birds sang in the wake of the storm. A band of ravens flew over them moaning like old men.

At the top of the rise, Jeremy squinted through binoculars down into the nest, scrutinised it tight-lipped and mumbled, 'She's fine. She's there, both nest-mates are fine.'

'Can I look?'

Jeremy passed the binoculars to her shaky hands. She could see the older brown and white eagle standing high on the nest looking straight at them, the two white younger eagles lay at her feet.

'She can see us better than we can see her,' said Jeremy.

Two rabbits lay on one edge of the nest, gutted and soaked now.

'You may not be the right person to ask, Jeremy, but do those rabbits look edible?'

'Gourmet quality.'

The river licked at the roots of the casuarina tree. The eaglet turned her head away, reached with her beak down over her shoulder, and preened the oil gland at the base of her tail. She pulled each tail feather through her beak and carefully spread oil through each one.

'She may put more stress on these adults,' said Jeremy. 'The male might have to catch larger prey, like hares and kangaroos, and kangaroos are a little too big for him to carry. So the female might have to hunt more than usual.'

'I should be at school, Jeremy.'

'Sorry, I'm rabbiting on.'

'It's late.'

They turned and hiked back over the hill.

They rustled through long grass that held last night's rain and soaked their shoes. On the way down the hill towards the car, he talked about birds because he couldn't help himself, about eagles and hunting and hares. Julia ducked behind a bush for the pee she hadn't time for before she left the house.

At school, late in the morning, Jeremy called her to the telephone and clasped his hand over the mouthpiece. 'Holly,' he whispered.

Julia took the receiver, 'Holly.'

Her voice was muted, like a shy child whispering over the phone. 'Those photographs.'

'Yes?'

'Cops said Lee's camera took them.'

Julia waited, listened to her own heavy breathing in the receiver. 'The ones of my house?'

'You have to watch out. He says the cops set him up, and you did too.'

'That's not true. Will you be all right?'

'Yes.' Her voice weak.

Holly told her in some detail about the two police visits. She spoke as if Lee's reaction and his welfare were the only things that mattered; her duty was to keep Lee happy.

Julia thanked her and asked her to call again anytime, then reassured her that she would guard the confidentiality of anything Holly told her.

Julia went to her classroom and faced Rose and lessons and boys all afternoon, used dreams of Kate like oxygen to carry her through the day.

In the grey anonymity of the Jamison Centre parking lot, she nosed her car against the brick wall and turned off the motor. The ground was scrubbed cleaned by last night's rain, but the wind had scattered pieces of eucalypt branches over the grass.

She was frightened of the place now, frightened of a parking lot, and started to shake as Kate rolled her Volvo in next to her. Julia hid her shaking hands, climbed into Kate's car and rode the few blocks over wet streets to her flat.

Julia wouldn't explain her shaking, wouldn't tell her that Lee had seized her and kept her prisoner. She realised how the fight now had taken on a menacing snarl, a beast with a life and body of its own that nobody could direct or limit. That morning, she had told Lisa about Lee and the knife. The police knew about Lee in the parking lot, and they would pursue him. This was police business and hopefully Kate would understand when Julia told her later. Lovers had a right to keep secrets from each other, and Kate knew that. Julia wondered how many days would pass before she could sit without trembling in Jamison.

Kate had even darker circles under her eyes than Julia.

Julia had never seen her look so haggard and old. Julia reached over and touched her, stroked her arm with the backs of her fingers. 'Did you sleep badly?'

She nodded. 'The storm.'

Kate said very little in the car, or after they arrived at the flat except, 'You'll have to excuse me today.'

They furtively watched her neighbours.

Julia looked around the flat, pushed some clothing aside and sat on the sofa, picked up a magazine and said, 'Holly phoned me this morning.'

Kate was distracted. 'Let's talk about it later.'

Julia glanced again at the neighbour's windows and Kate said, 'Don't worry, they should be away.

Kate made coffee and they sat on ladder-backed chairs at the kitchen table, silent at first.

Julia looked around the flat again and tried to be courteous. 'You've been able to bring some of yourself here.'

Kate sipped her coffee. 'I don't need anyone to judge my house-keeping.'

'Do you want to tell me about last night?' said Julia.

She said nothing at first, and sipped her coffee. She didn't look up. Then she said, 'The storm blew up around eleven, I think.'

'Yes, all over Canberra.'

She talked like she was reading a gothic novel. 'Branches slapped at my window all night, and they kept me awake. You see, that was the third night I hadn't slept, and my head was populated by these evil characters, one in particular. The harder I tried to fall asleep, the further I fell away from it.' She looked up, as if pleading for Julia to understand, but then looked past her. 'You see, it feeds on itself when you've gone some days without sleep. The dementia begins to eat you.'

Julia nodded slowly.

'But I understand it,' she said. 'I can supervise it, even write about it clinically. I can defeat it most nights, dig my heels in like a goat, resolute and stubborn enough to ride out the chaos in my head. But I can only do that for a certain number of nights. Walking around the house muttering to myself and pleading, "Go to sleep. Why can't you go to sleep." You know things are bad then, when you walk around the house talking to yourself and monitoring your own descent into hell.' Kate looked up, maybe trying to gauge Julia's reaction, then back down.

Julia sipped coffee. She knew Kate so well, yet she didn't, and was surprised, uneasy with this strange idiom. 'Go on,' she said.

'I tried to drive the faces away so I could sleep, but all the while branches rasped against the outer wall. Sleep was this dark hole, all that scratching dragged me away. I switched the light back on and looked around at the storm against the window. I picked up a copy of *The Australian Psychologist* and stared at it for an hour trying to read. I couldn't read it, just stared at an article about personality sorting with the Myers-Briggs. Then I saw myself from above rise up from the bed, put on a shirt and shoes and jeans and rush into the storm.'

'You were out in the storm last night?'

'Yes, I think so. The rain stung my face. It cooled me and calmed me a little. I charged down Wangara Street. Lamps over my head were yellow in the rain. There was no traffic at that hour, no people or animals out there, only grey windows and people behind white curtains out of the storm. You think about families in warm places, and lovers curled up under feather doonas in warm houses. I made it to the gate at the top of the rise.'

'Black Mountain.'

'The rain pelted me, like a beast slapping my face. I was hot. Away from any street lamps now, running through the dark, I stood with my mouth open and let the rain trickle into my cupped hands. I slipped on a muddy path, reached down and spread my fingers in the mud, and sat for a moment, salt and rain poured into my eyes and mouth. Then I stood up and ran. I didn't feel too bad. Glimpses of the moon slid by and spread my shadow like fingers over rocks and bushes. Bursts of lightning as bright as day. I wanted the darkness to swallow me. Can you understand that? I wanted to be swallowed.'

Julia waited for her to finish. She thought it would be a mistake to lie, so she nodded. 'I think so. I'm not sure.'

'I charged down the gully, burst through dark owl spaces in the trees.' She seemed to exclude Julia from her vision, reliving the storm, or the way she remembered it, the cold rain, her ability to see in darkness. 'Up past our pine tree. I looked hard and you weren't there. Further up the hill, I passed a tangled silver kite hanging in the top of a tree, with a painted red face on it that smiled at me and slapped against the tree in the wind. On top of the ridge, a southerly blasted rain against my back. I spread my arms and legs.

'Down the other side of the ridge, I came to our native cherry and stopped there and dropped to my knees and crawled under the tree, like visiting an empty church, curled there in the cold. I began to doze. It was dry under the tree but I was soaked and chilly, and sweating at the same time. I slept and thought I heard children playing outside. After a time, I lost the heat from my climb and could feel the ground and started to shiver, cold fingers poking into my back, like somebody reviving a corpse. I couldn't stop shivering.

'When I opened my eyes, I could see slivers of night and moon leaking through the top of our shelter, but clouds folded over it and I pulled aside the bough and lunged into the storm. Further along the ridge, I ran against the weight of the storm until I reached a tall stringybark that swayed and whipped on the hilltop. I fought the wind.' She looked down.

'Then the strangest thing happened. I looked further down the hillside, down through the canopy onto whipping branches and leaves below me. Lightning hit the mountain and lit the ground. I saw this form, a pale shape that I couldn't see clearly because the rain poured into my eyes. My eyes burrowed through darkness until I could see the outline of a clear-grey mare standing with its head down, head away from me in the storm. Its hindquarters and back took the force of the wind and rain, her tail whipped between her legs. She stood with one hip higher than the other, one hoof tipped back, resting her leg off the ground. Ears laid back, her head was low to the ground.

'I watched her, and put my hand up to protect my eyes from the sting, but the bandage on my finger slapped my face. The same grey rain poured into my eyes that poured down her forelock. With some pain, the mare raised her head and looked at me. Her eyes were liquid, shining black. I yelled at her, maybe I screamed at her. But my voice seemed to disappear as it left me.'

Julia watched her shivering in the chair, and said, 'It's from the photo in your office, darling, the photo of your niece and nephew, and the mare at their farm. I wonder if you need some sleep.'

Kate nodded. 'Yes, I need some sleep.'

Julia took her hand. 'Come on.'

Kate was undressed and in bed when Julia came upstairs. Julia undressed and climbed in beside her, reached over and pulled Kate towards her, with her bandaged hand to one side. Julia slid her hand down Kate's back, kissed her mouth. Kate was tired and pensive; she fell asleep curled into her.

Julia lay with her, felt her deep breathing, and her terrible dreams as she moaned and rolled onto her side.

Kate tucked into the wall and Julia held her there, and soon lay asleep against her back. After half an hour, she woke and could feel Kate's heavy, deep breathing, and the warmth of her strong back curled against her.

Kate's eyes opened and she lay watching the ceiling; she didn't seem to understand where she was. She reached over and touched Julia's face. She gently pulled Julia's hand from between her legs, stroked her, and Julia came. Holding her face on the pillow, Kate whispered, 'I love you.'

Kate held her.

30

Lovers

Tall red numbers on the clock set next to the pillow read 5.30 and Kate lay asleep. Julia pulled the sheets aside, put her bare feet onto the cold floor and padded quietly to the door.

Kate turned over, blurry-eyed and croaky. 'Are you leaving?'

'I have to go.'

'Let's go for a walk.'

'A short one,' said Julia. Naked and exposed, Julia pulled on her clothes.

She noticed a long honey-coloured strand of hair on the pillow and picked it up. She held it to the window and saw how the light caught its red tint, as if it held the heat of the afternoon sun. Running a gallery of mug shots through her brain of women in the Psychology department she stopped on the face of Rosemary Petersen, a strawberry blonde who sat next to Kate during meetings. A trained psychologist with powerful management skills, she had a bland, uneventful face, soft-featured and unthreatening. She had always struggled with her weight, but worked hard at the university gym and probably saw Kate there. She had eventually married a scruffy, bearded lecturer in the zoology department.

Julia held up the strand. 'What's this?'

Kate was dark-eyed and ghostly; she looked up and shook her head, 'Not now.'

Julia finished dressing, trying to bury her rage. Kate was right, of course, there was more than a little hypocrisy here. Accusing Kate of faithlessness when Julia was married and slept with a man, the duplicity of it. She wanted to understand the deep loneliness that Kate concealed at work and battled with each night. Julia wanted to see her own hypocrisy for what it was. But she couldn't.

On the street, Julia dampened the pain from the sharp images that stayed in her head, another woman sleeping in the bed they'd just left. She struggled and grimaced, inadvertently shook her head once. Julia knew she wouldn't talk about it, so she displaced the hurt.

'Holly phoned me this morning.'

'You told me,' said Kate.

'I know I told you. Do you want to hear this, or not?'

Kate frowned. 'You were told to stay away from her.'

'You should have thought about that before you drove me to Giralang.'

'Fine then, blame me.'

'The police took photographs with Lee's camera, and they matched photos taken of my house. The shots of Claire and Ben came out of Lee's camera, and I'm not sure why he fooled Lisa so easily.'

Kate smiled. 'People are easy to fool, especially if they're educated. Just cry out, "I'm the real victim here," and you're off the hook.'

'It's in police hands now. When they fronted him and told him they had to keep his camera, he went berserk, said he needed the camera for pig-hunting. He yelled and swore at the police, even threatened to call the newspapers if they didn't give it back.'

Kate looked puzzled. 'Why did he give up his camera so easily in the first place?'

'It's not against the law to take pictures of someone's house. He probably knew that. He didn't threaten me over the phone or write anything on the photos. Lee believes his own fairy tales and he's been stuffing people full of lies for so many years now he can't tell lies from reality. The truth is blurry in his head.'

Kate was quiet. A rippling sheet of starlings came over, travelling to a roost.

'Holly's scared,' said Julia.

'Yes.'

Down through Aranda they'd been quiet, nervous about walking open streets. On Black Mountain they had shelter and trees, and people were scarce.

After a time, Kate turned to Julia. 'I couldn't get that Dwight Yoakam song out of my head.'

'What?'

'The one about "two doors down".'

'You're going to tell me you bought it.'

'I did.'

'Well, don't play it for me today.'

She smiled faintly. 'I won't.'

Julia stopped on the grass. She realised what she hadn't realised before. 'You knew him, didn't you?'

'Who?'

'Lee.'

'Did it look like I knew him?'

'I said, you knew him.'

She looked away, as if stalling. Then she said, 'Yes, I knew him.' Again she looked ahead, stubborn with her secrets. 'I knew him, sort of. Not really him, I knew his father.'

'The father who adopted Lee.'

Kate walked ahead, like a shadow. She said things without looking up. 'He's adopted, and he's not adopted. He's adopted according to law, but he was given up at birth by a teacher in the country. She wanted the pregnancy kept secret, never wanted it found out, so yes, he was adopted, but no, he's not really adopted because he is John's son. Or so the story goes.'

'Why all the deception?'

'John Cavanaugh was a womaniser of the worst order, a teacher-fucker. They said he had a spanking room at the back of his office in the department. He used his position as inspector of schools to get his hands on as many female teachers as possible, remove as many pairs of knickers as time permitted. This unwed teacher from the country put her child up for adoption. John got his wife, Marge, to agree to take the child because the child was his. Well, like I said, that's the story. It was small-town gossip. Why him, why that particular child, I don't know. Because John Cavanaugh had others around.'

'Lee was the chosen one.'

'Yes, the chosen one. After Lee started fighting with John, and John tried to crush him, Lee changed from the shiny university prospect to a dingy plumber, pushed that plumber persona into John's face. Some people in town think Lee changed because he learned the truth and couldn't forgive John. None of us know where his mother is, of course, or who she was. I was told that an iron-clad deal was struck between John and Lee's biological mother, a signed promise to keep her identity secret.'

'This was common knowledge in town?'

'Amongst teachers it was. Staffroom gossip. And there's speculation that Lee's biological mother is in Western Australia or in the Northern Territory. Gone anyway. Nobody knows for certain where she is.'

'But you knew Lee at school?'

'Everybody knew him. I was two grades below him, so he didn't know me. But John Cavanaugh knew us. John and Marge Cavanaugh used to pass my father and mother in the street, say hello to the simple mechanic and his simple kindy-teacher wife and their simple daughter Kate, and my little brother. My father went sort of glum when John stepped up to us in the street, very quiet. John would put his arm around my father's shoulder, sort of grin at my mother, like they shared a private joke. He would say to my father, "How are ya, Ben? Nice to see you." Mother would look away and try to move on, but John played the friendly boss to my mother, like he was saying to my father, "Now, Ben, don't think for a moment that you have to stay here and talk to me, just because I'm smart and you're not so bright, or because I'm your wife's boss and a powerful man in town and you're a failure." Sure, my father was a failure. He knew that better than anyone. But he was a simple, good man – cornered.'

'You're saying that John knew you, but Lee doesn't know you.'

'John did that sort of thing to a lot of women in town, acted friendly in the street. Not just my parents. It was a sport that he loved. But that was John. I doubt if Lee knew who I was. In high school, two years is a big gap. I was the kid.'

Her words leaned over them, pressed down as they trudged over the oval. Julia said nothing because she would have fumbled any words. The raw grieving in Kate's throat, the sadness in her voice and the melancholy in the tilt of her head.

'I've talked enough about Lee and John. It doesn't bear thinking about. Some men destroy you if you draw attention to their defects, and John Cavanaugh was that kind of man. In a small town, you learn that lesson quickly.'

'And Lee never learned his lesson.'

'A beating is one thing, denial of birth is quite another.'

Kate was quiet, then said, 'Families are dangerous. Even when you leave them.'

They turned into a light breeze and drifted. They had learned the habit of repose. But Kate's silences frightened Julia more than her words. Julia feared Kate's dreams of leaving. She wanted to walk with Kate when they had brown coins of age on their faces, and their work had finished and children would visit them on holidays.

She felt low sun on her neck as they walked over the oval. Leaves hung like knives. She watched the bandage swing back and forth on Kate's finger and Julia's hands were cold now. She didn't want Kate to feel the chill in her fingers and pushed them deep in her pockets.

On the playground, Kate sat on a children's swing, rocked herself back and forth watching people walk by, listening to rosellas chattering in branches and laughing children or voices in her head. Kate spoke at the ground. 'The devil's at work here, and we need to make certain he's not us.'

They could smell wet grass, and Kate rocked in the swing with her bandaged hand off the chain. For a long time, they couldn't think of much to say, and blue dusk fell around them.

31

Night in Rose's House

Roaring in the house.

Lee started the fight, screaming down her mother, slurring his words and crashing his fist into the kitchen table. 'I told you. Keep those cunts away from my house.'

'I tried.'

'You sent for them.'

'No.'

'Fucking cow,' he screamed. 'You and the bitch told stories about me.'

Rose huddled under blankets in her bed and wondered if her sisters heard, or if the neighbours heard. He was getting drunker now and he would soon start beating her.

'Tell them you made it up. Tell them I never laid a hand on her.'

Holly waited, still hunched. She backed away from his rancid breath.

'*Tell them.*'

'We never made it up.' She stood and exposed herself to Lee's delirium.

'I swear, I'll kill you. Tell them it was lies.'

'I told them.'

Rose heard the determination hard in her mother's throat. It frightened her. The more Holly stood up to Lee, the more he would slap her face and punch her back as she cowered on the floor.

Lee crowded in close, towering above her, hops stinking on his breath made Holly crawl backwards. Spittle and beer flew onto her T-shirt.

Rose lifted the covers with shaking hands, got out of bed and stood at the door, barefoot in her nightgown.

'I'll cut you both. I'll cut you.'

Holly was quiet.

'You made me do this.'

'No,' said Holly.

Then it was silent.

'Why? Why're the cops doing this?'

'I don't know,' she said, small, sitting on the floor, looking down and rocking forward and back.

'You lied to them.'

'No.'

'Who'd believe you? You lie all the time. You're fucking against me too.'

'I didn't talk to them.'

'The cops took my camera.'

More silence, Rose shivered.

'*Answer me.*'

No answer from Holly.

'Answer me.'

Holly stood up against Lee's rising black menace.

'You gave my camera to the teacher. '

'I didn't.'

'Then to her girlfriend.'

'No.'

'Who then? Who'd you give the camera to?'

Silence.

'You gave it to Rose.'

'Leave her out of this.' Holly's voice in the bare light was nearly resolute.

'Tell me she didn't take them.'

'What good would that do?'

'Tell me the little bitch didn't take those photos. *Tell me.*'

'Okay, she didn't.'

'Let's ask her.'

Rose lifted the covers with a shaking hand and slipped out of her room, across the hall into the laundry. She squatted low on cold tiles at the back door, reached up and twisted the metal lock. It squeaked. Chilly air seeped in. Still and quiet. A thin moon, newly risen, poured shadows into the backyard and Lee would come looking for her now.

Then Rose heard her mother's taunt. 'What if I did? You bash the girls, and me.'

'Fuckin' liar. Never touched my girls.'

'You weren't too brave around that Kate.'

Rose, crouched at the back door, shaking and chilled, she wanted to run into the kitchen and stop her mother. But she turned to the open laundry door and escape into the backyard. But she froze.

Lee exploded. A glass broke, chairs clattered on the linoleum floor. Past Rose, still crouching low by the washing machine, he stumbled, heavy-legged down the hall.

'I warned you.' He rushed into her bedroom and groped around, found the empty bed. 'Where the fuck is she?' He stomped down to his own room, ripped through clothes in the closet, threw out shoes and a vacuum cleaner, walking boots and a cartridge vest until he found what he wanted. Then he stumbled out of the bedroom into the kitchen.

Rose wanted to run, but she crouched in the laundry.

Holly pleaded, 'No. Please, no.'

BANG. The loud crash through the house, bouncing off fibro walls, Debbie and Deedee screaming now, the last pig dog booming in the backyard.

Rose leapt from her crouch near the washing machine and darted to the kitchen. Her mother lay face down on the floor, sprawled with both feet turned in, twisted and still, her palms turned up, the pale skin against the floor, and her brown hair in a halo of blood. Lee stood looking down at Holly, the rifle hung in his hand. The Rottweiler barking in the backyard, Rose slid through to the front hallway, low, creeping.

She waited, picked up the phone, punched seven numbers in and waited for the click at the other end, 'He's killing us.'

Lee burst in from the kitchen rushing to the other side of the sitting room. 'You.'

'No,' Rose screamed, and dropped the receiver.

Down the hall, Deedee crying from her cot, louder now, 'Mummy,' and then Debbie.

Bleary-eyed and dazed, he turned at the little girls' screams. Muddled. Holly sitting up on the floor now. He aimed the rifle across the room at Holly's white face.

Rose ducked around the corner, low and creeping through the hallway into her bedroom, grinding her teeth, she slipped, banged her jaw against the bedpost, felt one of her front teeth crack. Leather boots pounding along wooden floorboards. Rose knew she was going to be killed.

'Stay there, bitch,' he slurred.

She lay between her bed and the wall. Lee pulled the door open, stepped into the blackened room and felt for the light switch. He couldn't find it. He moved into the room, hunting, trying to adjust his bleary eyes to blackness. Rose exploded over the bed, dashed to the doorway. Lee stretched, grabbed at her, brought the rifle up to smash into her frail bird bones. She burst through the open door running.

Swinging the gun from his left hand to the right, he turned and stumbled down the hall.

Debbie screaming in her cot, Deedee crying, '*Mummy.*'

Rose struggling with the front door, twisting the squeaky lock, pulling the door open as Lee came around the corner and raised the gun. She fell to the floor – BANG – the bullet ripped past her, shattering the glass in the front door.

Up and frantic now, crashing through jagged points of glass left in the door, ripped the hem of her nightgown, caught on a splinter, Lee staggering towards her. Rose pulling at her nightgown, crying, struggling, ripped it free as Lee grabbed her wrist. Lee had her now.

She turned, bit deep into his dirty knuckles, tasted his blood.

He yelled, '*Fucking…*' and dropped the gun to reach his bitten hand.

She twisted, vicious in her escape.

Sobbing, she ran into the dark street, down the block under street lamps with angry dogs barking up and down in neighbouring yards. She glanced over her shoulder and saw Lee running through shadows, shambling drunk, with the gun dangling from his right hand.

She wiped her nose and cheeks with the back of her hand, running down the middle of the street, air as cold as metal, onto a front lawn, she didn't know whose, around past the side of the house to a fence, she grabbed the top board, pulled herself up and flipped over into the backyard. Across the lawn to a high fence. She rushed to it, pulled herself up and threw one leg over. A deep growl, vicious dog barking and snarling as it leapt onto the side of the fence and snapped at her dangling foot. She pulled her leg up from the snarling, demented animal and dropped back into the other yard. She was trapped now.

Rose stood for a moment in the dark, peered around the backyard, then scurried low, like a sneaking cat into shadows at the back of the house. Walls crawling with shadows. She stood next to the step. On her belly, she edged under the concrete step, pushed aside tools and rubbish, curled and foetal in leaves and mud. She panted grey vapour into the space under the porch and tried to lay still. In the blue-black night, she waited for Lee with her face in the dirt.

He ran round the corner of the house in the part light, stumbled to the grass, down on all fours, pushing the rifle butt into the ground like a crutch and rose to his feet, stood for a moment, then ran to the fence. He started to climb over, slipped down, then put his hands on the top board and pulled himself over. Into the backyard now, with Rose.

Standing on grass, swivelling his head and scanning the yard, he walked to the opposite corner with his gun swinging from his right hand. He paced along the back fence, hunting. He looked under a bush. He stood high on his toes, wavering and looking over into the next yard.

The dog snarled, slammed against the fence. Lee jumped backwards, stood for a while and waited for the dog to stop barking. Then he listened.

In the backyard with Rose, he searched the ground, shambled along the back fence to the corner of the yard, looked under more bushes, trying to find where she lay. He walked up to the shadowy house and the porch, brushed against it with his leg, looked along the wall and along the fence. He turned away from the porch, like he might leave. Rose, dead still with her face in the mud, eyes wide and black, watching the heels of Lee's boots and the tip of his rifle.

He turned and faced the porch. Pointing the rifle into the dark space, he squatted and looked in. Lee pulled aside sheets of plastic and lawn tools, a shovel, and poured moonlight into the space under the porch. He bent and looked again, put his free hand out to feel in the dark, grabbed a handful of mud and poked his rifle barrel into the space, with his finger on the trigger. He felt a soft body; he poked her again with the rifle tip and reached in with his free hand.

A voice behind him. 'Lee.'

He turned and looked. A shadow coming towards him.

The shot rang through the neighbourhood.

32

Lisa Charles

Dogs yipping all over Giralang.

Officer Lisa Charles stood at the curb and waited for Rose's long cry to float towards her. A light wind cooled the sweat on her face. She motioned to Officer Nigel Plant, 'Go back and stay with them at the house.' She jogged down the dim street and listened.

Heart tearing inside her chest. Lights switching on in windows around the neighbourhood. Lisa beat her way across a thin strip of yard, watching shadows, peering over the back fence into a thin yellow haze cast from a porch lamp. Nothing. Lacy brown moths fluttering through wedges of light. Back on the street, she ran down the curb, jumping from her own running shadow tossed over the road by a street lamp.

She stopped, head bent in the middle of the street. Dogs yapping and nobody stepping onto their porches to quiet them. She looked hard into corners. At the end of the street through a silver mist, a little park scattered with giant yellow box trees. She walked closer, looking in the gloom at a rumpled form, like a bag of trash, or a person sitting on the ground with his back against a tree.

She stepped off the road onto wet grass, watching the body, easing towards it, maybe a dead man slumped cross-legged on the ground with a rifle across his knees. Or maybe not.

She stopped, unclipped her pistol. 'Lee?'

Nothing.

She walked closer, twenty metres away, head down and guarded, watching the body. She drew her handgun. 'Lee?' She paced a slow direct line towards the black form until she stood at the side of the tree, wondering if Lee had poked the barrel into his mouth and blasted his brain and the back of his head into the tree. She held up a torch above and away from her thinking she would see pink brains on the trunk. She looked down and watched the gun barrel. 'You all right, Lee?'

No answer.

In the pale glimmer of street lamps, she saw the withering spent reflection in his eyes, a look she'd seen many times after a creature had died.

'Lee?' She waited.

No movement.

She stepped closer and crouched with the pistol two-handed in front of her. 'Lee?'

The man raised his head with a steady unflinching look. His voice was flat. 'Are you going to shoot me?'

She hesitated for a moment, pointing the handgun at his face, watching the muzzle of Lee's gun. 'No. I'm not going to shoot you. Put the gun down in front of you.'

Lee studied the open throat of the gun pointed at him, looked down again, cross-legged and relaxed with his back against the tree, rifle across his lap.

'Lee, put the gun down.'

Finally he said, 'She phone you?'

'Who?'

'You know.'

'Holly, you mean?'

'No, Rose.'

'No, she didn't phone me. Somebody else phoned me.'

'Who did Rose phone?'

'It doesn't matter, Lee. Please put the gun down.'

He sat.

'Give me the gun, Lee.'

He looked up at Lisa as if he'd woken from a deep sleep, or calmed from the delirium of hatred that had driven him into the park.

She tried, with the handgun pointing at Lee's face to show calm in her expression, a comrade not judging him. 'It's all right. Nobody wants to harm you.'

He laid his hand on the rifle, hooked his finger into the trigger guard of the gun sitting in his lap.

'Lee, please put the gun down.'

He sat.

'It's all right. I won't shoot you.'

He didn't move.

Lisa waited. 'Lee?'

He laid the gun on the ground.

Lisa reached down with her handgun aimed at his face and looped her finger through the trigger guard, yeasty fumes of beer pricked her nose and she lifted the rifle off the ground. She stood with both guns and watched him.

He gazed up at her for a moment, then nodded. 'Sit down.'

'No, I'll stand, thanks.'

'Sure?'

'Quite sure.'

He rested his head back against the jagged brown trunk and closed his eyes.

During a brief sleep, Julia dreamed about walking through red sand hills and blue-bush with Marlene in sun-hardened country. She woke and waited until dawn with her head full of intolerable pictures. Stars dropped out one by one. In early light she rushed to her car and sped along Belconnen Way. Her eyes scratchy and raw from sleeplessness, her brain jittery from coffee. The shock in the night had robbed her voice, a weight on her chest, her mouth tasted like it was full of copper coins. She was unwashed, and would remain so all day. A blue and white police car sat on the grass in front of the school.

Lisa Charles, in uniform, was talking. She stopped and tried to smile as Julia came in, but it was a short smile that turned serious and consoling when she looked back at Jeremy. '...and I'm sorry that you had to go through all this. I hope you can understand that our hands were tied. We needed some corroborating evidence to show he was threatening or abusing a child, or in this case,' she looked at Julia, 'threatening you. I wish we didn't need to be so guarded, that we could arrest these men more easily, be less paranoid about mistrials and charges laid against the police. But that's the way things are these days, and the laws won't change soon.'

'Can you tell us what happened?,' said Julia.

'Part of it, I can tell you part of it. I'm expecting a call from the hospital and we need to notify next of kin. I can tell you that it's alleged that he started a fight with Holly, and the fight escalated. He took a rifle from his room, a pig gun, to threaten Holly and Rose. In a rage, apparently, the police allege that he shot Holly. Whether this was intentional or accidental, we can only speculate. Rose saw her mother lying on the kitchen floor after she'd been shot.'

It felt like a hammer blow to her stomach. Julia tried not to weep into the tissue over her mouth. 'She's dead?' Julia whispered.

'Holly crawled through the broken glass door, cut herself badly, but wandered down the street after Lee chased Rose into somebody's backyard. We found Holly in the street. As I said, I'm waiting for a call from the hospital.'

'And Rose?'

'She's in Calvary as well, in shock. Badly frightened by seeing all this.'

'He was drunk,' said Ruth.

'Let's wait on that,' said Lisa.

Julia looked at Jeremy's impassive face as he tried to speak.

His fingers were tangled in his lap, massaging each other. 'And Lee?'

'There's a park in Giralang, down the road from the house. I found him there, sitting on the ground with his back against a tree. A strange sight it was. Officer Nigel Plant stayed at the house. Roger Bomford, my sergeant, backed me up. We expected trouble, a siege maybe, but

Lee didn't struggle or even argue. He gave me the gun, stood up and came quietly.'

Julia said, 'This blew up over the photographs, didn't it?' She felt like a guilty child before judging adults.

'Not entirely. But Rose told us about the photographs. Lee told Holly to develop the film from his last pig hunt. Two shots left in the camera, so Rose asked if she could take them. She made her way to your house and took them.'

Julia was shaking, light-brained with hunger.

'Rose kept the prints for a while, then decided to put them in an envelope, take the bus over to your house, and leave them in your mailbox.'

'But why?'

'The notes in the letter box about Lee's dogs gave Rose the idea. When it blew up, Holly didn't know what to do, she froze. She couldn't tell Lee because he'd beat her, and beat Rose. They waited for a miracle, hoped it would fix itself.'

'It didn't,' said Jeremy.

Lisa stared at him. 'Obviously.'

Jeremy looked at Rose's desk in the corner. 'What's happening to the kids?'

'Lee's parents John and Marge are here.'

'In Canberra?'

'Yes. We've spent time with them and all three girls will go to Bathurst. We need to question Rose further. And I need to ask you some things'

Julia tightened. 'Go ahead.'

'The dead phone calls.'

'Yes?'

'They may have been from Rose. She had your number.'

'She made the phone calls?'

'We think so.'

Julia looked down again.

'She phoned once to hear your voice. She couldn't build up the courage to speak to you, and you shouted "Lee" into the phone.'

Julia felt nothing in the betrayal, listening through haze in the room.

'She grew up sneaky, hiding things from Lee, and she hated him. It turned into a convoluted mess, she lost control of it, and she didn't know what to do.'

'How did she get my number?'

'It's written on your dog's collar. She copied it into her notebook.'

'So Lee knows this.'

'He does now. He suspected it for some time. Suspected it was Rose, or Kate making the phone calls, and that one of you killed his dog.'

'One of us?'

Lisa nodded. 'Rose didn't admit to it. We still don't know for certain who it was, but I have a pretty good idea.'

The phone rang. Jeremy answered, 'Yes,' and handed it to Lisa.

She looked out the window. 'Yes. Yes. Okay. Thank you.' She hung up and turned to the group.

'Holly is serious, but alive.'

Ruth said, 'Good.'

'Julia, I need to ask you, and I'm sorry to do this, but I need to ask all of you – did you know that Kate Selby was seeing Rose?'

Julia looked up.

'Some days after school, they went for walks, and on some days the girl went to Kate's house.'

Julia shook her head.

'We know from neighbours that she visited more than once.'

Lisa looked at Julia and waited. Julia shook her head slowly. 'No. Rosemary Petersen, a woman in Kate's department visited, not Rose. There's some confusion.'

'We don't know about anyone visiting Dr Selby except Rose Cavanaugh, and you of course.' Lisa waited, but Julia didn't look up.

'Maybe it was a mother-daughter thing, we don't know. We don't know what their relationship was.'

Julia continued to look down and thought about the times that Kate warned her not to come to her house because neighbours would see. It wasn't because of neighbours.

'She walked on some nights, Kate did, or drove to Giralang and watched the Cavanaugh house. Rose had her number, and Kate wasn't far away when Lee started shooting.'

Julia tried to speak. 'I knew Kate went for walks up Black Mountain, down bike paths in Cook and Aranda.'

'And to the Cavanaughs' house in Giralang. Rose sneaked out one night and saw her.'

'I don't understand.'

'We don't totally understand either. We may never know the whole story.'

'But where was Kate last night? Why didn't she answer her phone?'

'Lee had Rose pinned down under a porch last night, in a backyard with the barrel of the gun poking into her spine, ready to shoot. Lee said that Kate emerged out of the dark behind them. He was confused about who it was, threatened by her when she stood her ground. Lee shot her. We don't know why, maybe Lee doesn't know why, but he left her on the ground and jumped over the fence, left the yard. Rose was kneeling on the ground with Kate when we arrived.'

'She's dead?'

Lisa nodded. 'I'm sorry.'

Julia saw Rose clearly, sitting on the ground with her hands in the gluey warmth of Kate's blood, crying and pleading to her.

They sat quietly in the room. Julia had curled in the chair with her face down on her knees.

Lisa shook her head slowly and said. 'It's one of the first things you learn in this job. The city is full of empty people trying to find each other.'

33

Winter Clothes

They stood with the wind in their faces. She followed Kate over rocks and left no tracks; she laid a hand on Kate's arm. A covey of choughs came by with spilled sugar on each wing.

They curled under a tree on soft grass, smelt clean and hot from the climb, with salt on their cheeks. Under branches scraping in the wind, she listened to whispered hopes, a secret flutter took possession and drowsiness fell over them. The city purred and shadows waved over their sleeping forms.

Kate woke and reached across and touched Julia's ear. 'You've lost an earring.' Kate searched the ground and pointed, 'Here,' poking her fingers through leaves and grass and handing it over.

Julia shook her head and smiled. 'Keep it.'

They turned and walked through candle bark woodland down the green flank of the mountain.

Headstones in that part of the cemetery lay at ground level with grass folded over the edges. After days of blue sky, the downpour came in sheets over the city, trickling down strips of bark in the arms of eucalypts, an afternoon with dark slanting rain. A tall metal canopy resting on wheels sheltered the dirt chamber and stopped water from pouring in. No flowers came from Lee's family; their capacity for doing good eluded them on the day.

Julia kept the earring in her pocket and visited each day, placed her hands in damp soil and wept.

That year, they dealt with other men like Lee. Some days, Ruth talked about Lee and vicious men like him. 'You'll see. This'll all stop in twenty years' time. It has to."

Rose didn't go to Bathurst with her sisters. For now, she stayed at Barnardo's. She came back to school, her face hollow-cheeked and stricken by all that had happened. Jeremy took her to the river and they stood on the escarpment for an hour and saw an eagle soaring over the nest tree. Both thought it was the eagle they'd saved, but nobody knew for sure. Rose never talked about the night in Giralang and was subdued when Julia spoke about Kate. She smiled sometimes, and Rose and Julia took long walks through woodland on Black Mountain.

A tight airless bond formed between them that made the boys uncomfortable.

Slanting light came through slats on the window onto Julia's lap. She ordered coffee, opened the envelope and read it again, laid the handwritten note on the table and tried to decide. The hurt crushing down.

She felt a wingbeat of breath on her neck as the door swung open and a girl of about twelve came in with a boy. The girl was loose and easy. She smiled and talked as she walked, a skinny high school kid in tight jeans, or maybe she was in Year Six. She didn't hold the boy's hand, but looked at him in small glances. Coy and excited, she waved her hands as she spoke.

Julia stirred her coffee and watched them, trying to decide if she was troubled or pleased, wondering if the girl would come to her one day with greasy hair and dirt under her nails and a back-story soaked in cruelty.

As they stood waiting, the boy rested his thumb on the girl's hip, slid his fingers into her back pocket. Julia watched the girl's back, and the curve of her neck, knew her warmth as the boy leaned into her.

After an hour, Julia stood, paid for coffee and left. She drove into the city, watched couples and imagined stories of their time spent loving where nobody could see them, in stretches of powerful calm, naked hours in secret.

She whispered, 'I forgive you.'

At home, she sat for an hour at the window, then stood and walked to her bedroom and laid out some winter clothes.